4.99   9-11-08

W9-BQZ-389

BEYOND THE SUNRISE

Something was stuck in Jody's mind — something about a new boat. She had a feeling it might be very important. "I want to go back to the inlet," she said, standing up abruptly from the table. "I think maybe I know som...

...self. "I ca... ...gain, m... ...t I've g...

JUV FIC BAG
Baglio, Ben M.
Beyond the sunrise

Snyder County Library
One North High Street
Selinsgrove, Pennsylvania 17870
Telephone: (570) 374-7163

Look out for more titles in this series

Dolphin Diaries ™

Ben M. Baglio

Illustrations by Judith Lawton

BEYOND
THE SUNRISE

SNYDER COUNTY LIBRARIES INC.
APPLE
PAPERBACK
ONE NORTH HIGH STREET
SELINSGROVE, PA 17870

SCHOLASTIC INC.
New York Toronto London Auckland Sydney
Mexico City New Delhi Hong Kong Buenos Aires

If you purchased this book without a cover, you should be aware that this book is stolen property. It was reported as "unsold and destroyed" to the publisher, and neither the author nor the publisher has received any payment for this "stripped book."

No part of this publication may be reproduced in whole or in part, or stored in a retrieval system, or transmitted in any form or by any means, electronic, mechanical, photocopying, recording, or otherwise, without written permission of the publisher. For information regarding permission, write to Working Partners Limited, 1 Albion Place, London W6 0QT, United Kingdom.

ISBN 0-439-44617-1

Text copyright © 2003 by Working Partners Limited.
Illustrations copyright © 2003 by Judith Lawton.

All rights reserved. Published by Scholastic Inc., 557 Broadway, New York, NY 10012, by arrangement with Working Partners Limited. DOLPHIN DIARIES is a trademark of Working Partners Limited. SCHOLASTIC, APPLE PAPERBACKS, and associated logos are trademarks and/or registered trademarks of Scholastic Inc.

12 11 10 9 8 7   4 5 6 7 8/0

Printed in the U.S.A.   40
First Scholastic printing, April 2003

Special thanks to Lucy Courtenay

Thanks also to the Whale and Dolphin
Conservation Society for reviewing the
information contained in this book

1

May 26 — Dawn — Dolphin Dreamer, Sundarbans Delta, Bangladesh

The sun has only just risen, and the whole river is beginning to change color. It was gray about five minutes ago, and now it's orange and red and pink — all the colors of the dawn sky. It's an incredible, beautiful sight.

All the fishermen have been working for nearly an hour already. Can you believe it? They are as quiet as anything. I don't think the fish really know that they are there. The otters don't make any noise, either. Yes, trained otters! I couldn't believe my eyes! I feel like the fishermen, Shiv, and I are the only people alive. It's magical.

Jody McGrath closed her diary and stood up. The deck of *Dolphin Dreamer* was cool and slightly damp under her feet as she walked across it as quietly as she could. The river lapped gently at the sides of the boat and the great mangrove trees stood, gnarled and twisted, at the water's edge in the dawn light.

Ten-year-old Shivam Kaushik looked around from his position by *Dolphin Dreamer*'s railing as Jody approached. He had suggested this early morning adventure yesterday at dinner. He and Jody had slipped out before sunrise to watch the fishermen at work. The deck of *Dolphin Dreamer* gave them a great view of the action.

"Have I missed much, Shiv?" Jody whispered.

Shiv smiled at her, his white teeth gleaming in the light of the rising sun. "Not much," he said. "Except Jafar's otter just swallowed one of his biggest fish. He wasn't very happy!"

Jody grinned back. The otters weren't supposed to

eat the fish. They wore special collars to stop them from swallowing anything too big. Jafar's otter must have lost his collar. Jody knew that she should sympathize with the fisherman because losing fish meant losing money. But she couldn't help feeling glad that the hardworking otter had sneaked a reward for all his work.

They watched the otters as they slid off the fishermen's brightly colored houseboats and into the smooth water of the river with hardly a splash. The sleek silver fish grouped together nervously just below the surface of the water — sensing the presence of hunters. The otters then chased the fish straight into the waiting nets. It was a wonderful sight.

The fishermen were now shouting, hauling their catches out of the water. They pulled them in, hand over hand, until the full nets of gleaming, wriggling silver and black hit the decks of their long, low, brightly painted boats. The catch was good that morning, Jody could tell.

The Sundarbans Delta was a maze of mangrove swamps and rivers in the Bay of Bengal. Part of the Sundarbans lay in India and the rest in Bangladesh. Hundreds of small rivers cut through the mangroves and down to the sea, most of them stemming from India's sacred river, the Ganges. It was a strange, watery world, and a UNESCO World Heritage site. And most important, it was home to a couple of rather unusual species of dolphin, though Jody hadn't seen any yet.

Jody's parents, Craig and Gina McGrath, were marine biologists. They and the rest of their team had arrived in the Sundarbans two days ago, aboard their boat, *Dolphin Dreamer.* They were all staying with Shiv's parents, Ravi and Sunnu Kaushik, at the Sukhi Rest House, a neatly thatched hut with a wide wooden veranda that stood a little way back from the river's edge, just behind where *Dolphin Dreamer* was moored.

The crew of *Dolphin Dreamer* had been sailing around the world for almost a year now, researching dolphins in their natural habitats. Jody knew how lucky she was to have been allowed to go on this trip. She felt like she had increased her knowledge of dolphins a thousand times over since leaving her home in Florida the previous June. She hadn't thought it was possible to love dolphins more than she already did, but she had managed it. The sight of a dolphin, even after nearly a year of seeing them in different places around the world, always filled her heart with joy.

Jody had made friends with Shiv, the Kaushiks' eldest son, almost as soon as they had arrived at the Sukhi Rest House. Although Shiv was two years younger than Jody, his English was good, thanks to a regular stream of English-speaking visitors, scientists, and researchers who stayed at his parents' rest house. He loved to talk to Jody about the wildlife of the delta, and he was so knowledgeable about the animals in the Sundarbans that Jody was learning something new from him every minute. He, in turn, enjoyed practicing his English with Jody and was eager to learn about the places she had visited and the dolphins she had seen.

Jody glanced at the net on the nearest fishing boat and frowned. "Shiv, these nets don't hurt the dolphins, do they?" she asked anxiously.

Jody knew that one of the greatest dangers to dolphins often lay with the kind of nets fishermen used. If the mesh was the wrong size, the dolphins would get caught and wouldn't be able to escape. Because they needed to breathe above water, they could sometimes even drown as the nets trapped them below the surface.

"The nets are safe," Shiv assured Jody. "And the fishermen would never hurt the dolphins. They believe that dolphins are sacred."

Jody was intrigued. "You mean, they worship them?"

"Not exactly," said Shiv. "But there are stories, you know? Fishermen love stories. I have grown up hearing stories of dolphins."

"What kind of stories?" asked Jody.

"I have heard of a river in India with a white dolphin," said Shiv. "The villagers say that the dolphin is really a young girl. She was in love with a young fisherman, but one day he drowned far out at sea. The girl cried so much that the river rose around her, and she became a dolphin. Perhaps she sees her fisherman now, down at the bottom of the sea."

"That's sad," said Jody after a moment. She pictured the lonely white dolphin in the river.

"We have happy stories, too," Shiv added. "South of

here, I have heard that dolphins help fishermen catch the fish, like otters!" He pointed at the otters, which were standing on the decks of the fishing boats, watching their owners sort the catch and waiting for their reward.

"Or sheepdogs," said Jody.

Shiv nodded. "I have heard of this," he said. "The dogs chase the sheep, yes?"

"They don't chase them!" Jody laughed. "At least, they aren't supposed to. They herd them."

"I have never seen a sheep," said Shiv. "I have seen pictures, though. They must be very hot in their wool coats."

"They often live in pretty cold countries," Jody pointed out. "They need their coats for the winter."

Shiv smiled and shrugged. For all his local knowledge, he knew very little about life outside the delta. He had spent his whole life in the Sundarbans, and all the information he had about other places in the world came from the few books his parents had in the house and the visitors he had spoken to. Jody knew that he found it difficult to understand the idea of really cold weather. In the Sundarbans, the mangrove swamps kept the air moist, and temperatures never fell below freezing. Most of the year the delta air was heavy, hot, and humid. Today was no exception.

"Maybe one day the dolphins in this river will help the Sundarbans fishermen," said Shiv hopefully. "I have never seen it, but if it happens in the south, it can happen here, I am sure of it. Today the catch was good, but I have seen days where the fishermen catch very little."

"Do you have white dolphins here in the Sundarbans?" Jody asked.

"I have never seen a white one," said Shiv. "We have Ganges River dolphins, which are gray. Also Irrawaddy dolphins."

Irrawaddy dolphins! These were the dolphins Jody was hoping to see. Her parents had told her all about them — they were famous for keeping to themselves. She had seen a few pictures of Irrawaddies, and she thought that they looked adorable. Their heads were blunt and rounded, without beaks, which made them look both friendly and faintly comical.

"Have you ever seen an Irrawaddy dolphin?" Jody asked eagerly.

Shiv nodded. "Of course," he said with a laugh. "But not many. Ganges dolphins and Irrawaddies are very rare."

A sudden worrying thought struck Jody. "Shiv," she said, "we're only staying for ten days, and we've already been here for two of those. Do you think we'll see an Irrawaddy?"

"Maybe," said Shiv. "You just have to look very hard. They don't often jump out of the river, so they are not so easy to see."

Jody remembered reading about the Irrawaddy habit of keeping below the river surface. Irrawaddies were totally unlike the bottle-nosed dolphins she'd seen, which happily leaped above the water for the world to see. She resolved to keep a very sharp eye on the river, just in case she caught sight of one gliding past. "They must come up to breathe," she said hopefully. "Maybe we'll see one breathing."

"It's possible," Shiv agreed. "But they like to be somewhere quiet and safe when they come up for air. You should be prepared not to see one, maybe. Then you won't be disappointed."

Jody frowned. The Irrawaddy sounded even more of

a challenge than some of the other notoriously shy dolphins she had managed to see over the past year. The Indo-Pacific humpback dolphin didn't show itself very often, although she had managed to make friends with one in Australia. And the river botos of South America had been very secretive as well. She knew that seeing a shy dolphin had a special thrill of its own, but she wished that it was a little easier. They had been lucky so far, but maybe the Irrawaddy would be the first dolphin to stay out of sight.

"It may not be so bad," said Shiv, relenting at the sight of Jody's thoughtful face. "The Irrawaddy is curious, like other dolphins. Sometimes they put their heads above the water, like this." He bobbed his head up to imitate a dolphin rising to the surface of a river to take a look around.

Jody laughed. "Like a seal!" she said.

"A seal?" said Shivam. "What is a seal?"

Jody explained. It was amazing to think that Shivam had never seen a seal, or even a picture of a seal. It struck her again just how lucky she was to be on this trip, traveling around the world and experiencing so much.

They both turned around when they heard footsteps behind them.

"You two are up early." Harry Pierce yawned, coming up the cabin steps to join Jody and Shiv on the deck.

Harry was the captain of *Dolphin Dreamer* and had decided to sleep aboard the ship while they were in the Sundarbans. When the McGraths had tried to persuade him to join them at the Sukhi Rest House, he had explained that he didn't sleep very well on dry land. He missed the rocking motion of the boat. Harry's daughter, Brittany, who was also on the trip, had no such problems. She had been the first off the *Dolphin Dreamer* when they had docked, and she had taken the best bed in the rest house. Unlike Jody, she wasn't a big fan of life at sea.

"Was it a good catch?" Harry asked, shading his eyes and looking out at the fishing boats.

"It seemed pretty good," Jody began.

Suddenly, the calm waters at the side of the boat began to bubble as something below the surface thrashed a huge tail. A flock of brightly colored birds rose from the mangrove trees in alarm, flapping their wings in a riot of color and noise.

"What's happening?" Jody asked in surprise.

The water calmed down again. Minutes later, it foamed around the base of the fishing boats and turned a murky brown. The fishermen yelled and ducked inside the cabins on the boats.

"Look!" Shiv suddenly shouted, pointing into the water.

Jody stared in horror as a long, dark body rose out of the river, opening a pair of huge jaws. A crocodile!

A crocodile causes chaos. . . .

2

May 26 — midday — upstairs in the Sukhi Rest House
I've never seen such a huge crocodile as the one we saw
this morning. It made the alligators back home in Florida
look like toys! It must have been as long as one of the
houseboats moored along the edge of the river. It gave us
such a shock. It managed to catch one of the nets, which
was still trailing in the water. We watched as it dragged
the net, with all its fish, back into the river. The fisherman
didn't stand a chance of pulling the net back on board. If
he'd tried, the croc would have pulled him overboard, too.
*   Shiv says the net belonged to Jafar — the same fisher-*

man whose otter ate the biggest fish. All in all, poor old
Jafar had a pretty bad day fishing.

Jody looked up from her diary with a yawn. Her bed
was very comfortable — she'd almost fallen asleep
halfway through her description of the morning she
had shared with Shiv and the fishermen. But she had
been determined to finish her entry before lunch.

The diary had been her father's idea. He had kept a
diary when he was a boy and had even won a compe-
tition with his writing. When they had left Florida the
previous June, he had suggested to Jody that she might
like to keep a special diary of all the places they visited.

A year later and the notebook was a little dirtier
around the edges, but it was steadily filling up. Jody
loved taking a little time every day to think about the
things she had seen and write them down. Her diary
had become like a friend, someone she could chat with
and confide in. She knew that when they returned to
Florida, it would be a fantastic reminder of the trip.

She put the diary down on the wooden bedside

table and stood up, breathing in the rich smell of the warm, wooden walls around her. She was sharing the room with Brittany. There was a fine-meshed mosquito net in the window, which faced away from the river, and two more nets draped around the beds. Brightly patterned curtains and a rag rug on the floor finished the picture, along with a wonderful, mysterious view of the dark and tangled Sundarbans forest out of the window. It was quite a change from the wide blue sea view from Jody's cabin aboard *Dolphin Dreamer.*

As she slipped her shoes on, Jody thought about the unlucky fisherman she and Shiv had seen that morning. Back home, losing a fishing net was no big deal. You just had to go to the nearest store and buy a new one. But here, it was very different. The fishermen made their own nets, which could take several days. Several days making a net meant several days without catching any fish. And no fish meant no money. Jody hoped that the fisherman didn't have a big family to feed.

From what Jody had seen, the Sundarbans people had a hard life. Most of them earned their living as fishermen, catching fish and shellfish. Others worked as woodcutters or honey collectors. Tourism was limited, the climate was wet and unpredictable, and the area was full of wild and dangerous animals. But somehow, the people were both cheerful and welcoming.

Jody made her way downstairs to join the rest of the family. The spicy smell of cooking rice reminded her that breakfast had been a long time ago.

Shiv greeted her with a broad smile. "Jafar has found his net," he announced as Jody came into the room. "It arrived on the bank, floating very near Jafar's boat. Chalaka didn't like the taste, I think!"

"Good!" said Jody with relief. Then she frowned. "Chalaka?" she asked curiously. "Is that the name of the crocodile?"

"*Chalaka* means 'clever' in Hindi," said Shiv's father. He was a slim, short man with dark wings of hair that fell neatly on either side of a part. In his arms slept three-year-old Ambika, the Kaushiks' youngest daughter. "That crocodile is very clever, so Chalaka is her name. The fishermen know her well. But I think she knows *them* even better!"

"Come and eat." Shiv's mother, Sunnu, beckoned

Jody to the table, where the rest of her family, plus Brittany, were sitting.

"It's about time!" said Jimmy with relief. "I'm starving!"

Jimmy was one of Jody's brothers and was permanently hungry.

"Me, too," said Sean, Jimmy's twin. "*Starving.*"

With their red hair and fair, freckled skin, the two eight-year-old boys looked very much like their father, whereas Jody took after her darker-skinned Italian mother, Gina.

"Sorry, everyone," Jody said, sitting down next to her mother. "I was writing about the crocodile Shiv and I saw this morning. You should have been there!"

"I couldn't get out of bed this morning," said Gina McGrath apologetically. "It must be our bed, Sunnu. It's the most comfortable thing I've slept in since we left Florida!"

Sunnu smiled at the compliment and placed a dish of rice on the table. Jimmy immediately reached for it, but Jody's dad was too quick for him.

"Oh, no, you don't," he said swiftly, batting away his

son's greedy fingers. "You can wait your turn like everyone else."

"Please, help yourself!" Sunnu laughed. She was a short, plump woman with slanting, almond-shaped eyes and a long, shining braid down her back. "It's good to see hungry boys."

"I'm glad I didn't see a crocodile," said Brittany Pierce with a shiver, reaching for the pile of warm, fragrant chapatis that had been placed in the middle of the table. "I would have screamed."

"You always scream," said Jimmy, and made a face at her. "Even at the tiniest creepy crawly."

Sean snickered.

"Ha-ha," Brittany said sarcastically, flipping her wavy blond hair back over her shoulders. "You are *so* not funny, Jimmy."

Brittany had joined *Dolphin Dreamer* at the last minute back in June, when her mother had unexpectedly gone to Europe on vacation. Harry Pierce hadn't planned on having his daughter along on the trip, but there had been no alternative. She had been a difficult member of the team from that first day, when she had made it very clear that she didn't want to be there. Even though she had changed a lot in the last year, she was still very easy to tease.

Jody looked around. "Where are the others?" she asked.

"Let's see," said Gina, counting on her fingers. "Harry's on the boat, as you know. Cam's with him."

Cameron Tucker was *Dolphin Dreamer*'s first mate and Harry's right-hand man.

"Mei Lin was invited to lunch by one of the fishing families today," Gina continued.

"I hope she gets a few recipes while she's there," Craig joked, reaching for the rice and piling it high on his plate. "With any luck, we'll get a few local dishes on the next leg of our trip."

Mei Lin Zhong was *Dolphin Dreamer*'s cook, though she had been an engineering student back in China, and was the boat's engineer, too.

"I have no idea where Maddie is," Gina admitted. "Maybe preparing your next algebra lesson." She winked at Jody and her brothers.

Jody, Sean, and Jimmy all groaned. They loved Maddie, their fun, young tutor, but algebra was algebra whether you were in Florida or Bangladesh.

"And . . ." Gina paused and frowned. "Oh, who have I forgotten?"

"Dr. Taylor," said Jimmy and Sean in unison.

"As if you could forget Dr. Taylor." Brittany sighed.

"Did somebody call?" A pink, balding head appeared around the door. Dr. Jefferson Taylor peered in from the veranda, blinking in the dim light. He was the representative of *Dolphin Dreamer*'s sponsor, PetroCo, and had been with the expedition from the beginning. "I was caught up here with what I believe is a gray-headed fish eagle." He waved a pair of binoculars to emphasize his point. "Just as well we found these," he said. "Though I must say, finding them in my laundry basket was a little unexpected. How they got there, I'll never know." He looked outside again. "Most rare, the gray-headed fish eagle," he muttered with satisfaction before vanishing from sight.

Jimmy and Sean burst out laughing. Jody couldn't help grinning, either. The Kaushiks' younger son, Ajay, had confessed to hiding Dr. Taylor's binoculars that morning. He had been sent up to his room more than an hour ago to think about what he had done. At seven years old, he was as naughty as the twins, and the three boys were already fast friends.

A moment later, Dr. Taylor reappeared. "I'm so sorry," he said. "I forgot to ask. Was I called in for a reason?"

Gina smiled at him. "Not to worry, Dr. Taylor. Lunch is here, when you feel like it."

"Most kind." Dr. Taylor nodded. "One does work up quite an appetite when bird-watching. Just one minute . . ."

And as if he were being pulled by an invisible string, Dr. Taylor disappeared outside again.

Lunch was almost over when an unexpected visitor arrived at the door.

"Harry!" said Gina. "I didn't think we were ever going to get you ashore! Would you like some lunch?"

Harry made a face and scratched absently at his beard. "I'm not hungry, thanks, Gina."

Jody saw that the captain was looking worried.

Craig noticed as well. "What's up, Harry?" he asked. "Is there a problem?"

"The *Dolphin Dreamer*'s engine has been leaking oil all morning," Harry replied. "I think we've got a problem with the carburetor."

"Oh, dear, can it be fixed?" asked Gina with concern in her voice.

The captain shook his head. "I don't think so this time. The carburetor is pretty much worn out after that long trek from Australia. Cam took a look and he agrees. We're going to have to replace it before we leave, or we could find ourselves stranded in the middle of the Indian Ocean."

"Don't we keep spare parts aboard?" asked Craig.

Harry nodded. "Of course. But unfortunately, we need more than just spare parts. I'm going to need to find a boatyard pretty fast, or we'll end up staying here longer than we planned. If we're still here when the monsoon season starts, well . . ."

He didn't need to finish his sentence. Monsoon weather, with its lashing rain and howling winds, was notoriously bad in this part of the world. Jody knew how important it was that they left the Sundarbans before the monsoons, or they could be stranded in Bangladesh for several months. It was vital that they kept to their schedule, or they could miss seeing certain species of dolphin altogether.

There was a brief, worried silence.

"Is there a boatyard near here, Ravi?" said Craig at last, turning to their host. "I mean a big boatyard, one that's equipped to fix major problems like this?"

"Not right here," said Ravi. "But you have seen the Sundarbans. Boats are a way of life to us. We depend on them for everything. So yes, we have some good boatyards." He thought for a moment. "I would suggest Mongla, perhaps. It is a three-hour journey up the Pusur River. Can your boat make a trip like that?"

Harry looked relieved. "I'm sure we have several more hours of use left in the carburetor if we don't push the engine too hard. I think we should head to Mongla in the morning."

"I will telephone ahead now to make sure that the

yard knows you are coming," said Sunnu. "Khaled is the owner; we know him. I am sure that he will be able to do the work for you."

"Thank you so much," said Gina with relief. "We really can't stay here into the monsoon season. Much as we'd love to stay in the Sundarbans for a few more months, Sunnu, we . . ."

Sunnu waved her hand. "I know. The world is a big place, and you must travel when you can. We would like to have you for longer as well, but monsoon season is a bad time. I think you wouldn't like the Sundarbans as much then as perhaps you do now!"

"Maybe you will see your Irrawaddy dolphin tomorrow," said Shiv as he guided his small wooden dinghy away from the Sukhi mooring that afternoon. "The Pusur is a great river, and many animals live in it. Three hours to Mongla and three hours back is plenty of time for you to look."

"I hope so," Jody said passionately. She looked at the swirling brown river that flowed around them. "I might even see an Irrawaddy now!"

"And if you don't see an Irrawaddy, I promise you will see plenty of other exciting things instead," said Shiv confidently.

He steered the boat into calmer water. He was taking Jody out to explore the mangrove forest. He had offered to take Brittany as well, but she'd taken one look at his small, battered dinghy and refused to set foot in it. So once again, he and Jody were on their own.

Because the forest was made up of many hundreds of small islands, the only way to travel was by boat. Jody loved the idea of sailing through a forest. It reminded her of the Orinoco River delta in South America, where the boto dolphins had sometimes swum among the tree branches when the river level was high enough.

Jody looked around her at Shiv's boat. It was a little shabby, but it was also watertight and surprisingly comfortable. "Does your dinghy have a name, Shiv?" she asked.

Shiv looked pleased at the question. "She is called *Big Ben*," he said proudly. "I have always wanted to see London and so I have a piece of London here at home with me."

"It's a good name." Jody smiled. "And London's a pretty good place, I hear. I'd love to go there someday, too."

They started talking about the places Jody had visited. Soon, they were so caught up in their conversation that Jody forgot to watch out for dolphins.

Suddenly, halfway through a conversation about the pilot whales in the Canary Islands, Shiv touched Jody's sleeve.

"Look," he said. "Fishing cat."

A large wildcat with spotted, olive-gray fur was crouched on the shore, watching them. Jody stared back with awe. The fishing cat's wild amber eyes glowed at them for a moment before it turned its attention to the river. Suddenly, it flashed a paw into the water and hooked a large, wriggling eel out with a powerful claw. With one final suspicious glance over its shoulder at Jody and Shiv, the cat slipped into the forest to enjoy its feast.

They saw plenty of other exciting things that afternoon, as Shiv had promised. Screeching monkeys swung over their heads through the narrower river

Fishing cat

channels, and long-legged river waders picked their way delicately along the muddy river shore. They even saw a sleeping python hanging among the branches of a tree. There didn't seem to be any crocodiles in this part of the river, Jody was thankful to see.

Suddenly, a rounded gray shape rose briefly out of the water, just ahead of the dinghy. It vanished again a second later.

27

"Shiv, I think that was a dolphin!" Jody said breathlessly, pointing. "Follow it, quick!"

The dolphin breached again very briefly. It was breaking the surface of the water for only a moment. Jody narrowed her eyes, trying to pick out a distinctive head shape. Was it an Irrawaddy?

They followed the dolphin's wake toward a small, mossy-looking island. It darted suddenly into one of a tangle of water channels, and Jody lost sight of it.

"It's OK," said Shiv, guiding the dinghy down the channel. "I think if we land, we will be able to follow it on foot."

They bumped gently ashore, beside a clump of tall, dark green bamboo, which rose up as straight and high as a building. Shiv lashed the dinghy to the gnarled stump of a mangrove tree and hopped ashore. Then he held a finger to his lips and beckoned Jody to cross the island with him, toward a water channel on the opposite side.

"Hey!" an angry voice shouted. "What are you doing? You should not be here. You must leave!"

A very tall, dark-skinned man was standing there, glaring furiously at Jody. Jody nearly leaped out of her skin at the sound of his voice.

The man took a step toward her. "Go away!" he said again, flapping his hands. "You are trespassing. Go away!"

Shiv stepped forward and asked the man a question in Hindi. The man replied in a furious burst of language, waving his hands and shouting. He was clearly very upset.

"Shiv, I think we should go," said Jody in a low voice, backing toward the dinghy.

Shiv turned to her. "This is not right," he said. "He does not own this land. He cannot tell us to leave."

The man was still shouting. He took a threatening step toward them.

Jody pulled at Shiv's arm. "Come on, Shiv," she said. "We can come back another day."

The man swung back to her. "No," he said clearly. "No other day. You must leave and not come back."

He obviously wasn't going to change his mind. Jody

pulled Shiv back to the dinghy, and they cast off. The tall man stood on the shore of the island and watched them leave.

"Don't think you can sneak back!" he shouted across the water. "I will speak to your parents, Shivam Kaushik. I want a promise that you will never trespass on my land again!"

3

Jody and Shiv found their parents sitting on the veranda of the Sukhi Rest House when they got back. Ajay and the boys were playing inside, and little Ambika was sitting at Sunnu's feet, playing with a doll and singing quietly to herself. Brittany was playing cards with Maddie, and Dr. Taylor was at the table making careful notes about the birds he had seen that day. Jody suddenly felt very glad to see so many friendly faces.

"Did you have a good trip?" asked Craig, looking up.

"Yes and no," Jody admitted, sitting beside him. "We saw a fishing cat, which was fantastic. And we spotted

31

a dolphin, but then we met this horrible man who chased us away."

"It was Mr. Vikram," Shiv explained to his parents. "He shouted at us because he said we were trespassing. But we were nowhere near his land."

"Shiv," said Sunnu, "remember, this is Mr. Vikram we are talking about. He doesn't follow the same rules as the rest of us."

"Why not?" Jody wanted to know.

Ravi swung thoughtfully on the veranda seat, which was piled high with creamy cushions. "Mr. Vikram is a neighbor of ours," he said. "He is a strange man, but you shouldn't worry about him. He has lived alone since his wife died last year, and he has become very solitary. We have learned to just leave him alone. Perhaps it is wisest for you to do the same."

Jody thought it sounded very sad. "Did he love his wife very much?" she asked.

"Yes," said Sunnu. "He did."

A strange noise from the depths of the forest made Jody turn her head. It sounded like a deep, throaty cough.

Ravi and Sunnu immediately stood up and looked out into the trees. Jody's parents did the same.

"What was that?" Jody asked curiously.

"Tiger," said Ravi, his eyes searching the forest.

Brittany shrieked and dropped her cards.

"It's OK," Sunnu reassured her. "It won't come to the rest house. But it might be better if we went inside, anyway."

Everyone obediently moved into the house.

"This place is so dangerous!" Brittany complained, throwing herself down on one of the sofas in the main living area. "First crocodiles and now tigers!"

"Tigers?" Jimmy asked with interest, looking up from his board game with Sean and Ajay. "Cool!"

"Not very cool if you are facing a hungry one, Jimmy," said Gina dryly.

"I faced a hungry tiger once," boasted Ajay.

"Yes — and the door was locked and the window was closed!" Sunnu teased, ruffling her younger son's hair.

"You may see tigers tomorrow on the way to Mongla," said Ravi. "There are maybe three hundred in the Bangladeshi part of the Sundarbans."

"And if you don't see the tiger," Sunnu added, smiling, "the tiger will most certainly see you. There is a saying in the Sundarbans: 'Here the tiger is always watching you.'"

"I don't mind if the tiger is watching," said Brittany, "so long as that's all it's doing."

"And what about dolphins?" Jody asked hopefully.

"I was about to ask the same thing!" Gina laughed. "We've been here for two days already, and we haven't laid eyes on the purpose of our visit."

"The *porpoise* of our visit," Sean quipped, and Jimmy collapsed into giggles.

A tall, blond young man stepped into the room and looked around. His loose linen clothes were streaked with paint, and he had a splotch of blue on his left cheek. "New guests, I see?" he said with a smile.

"Philip, at last you are here!" Sunnu exclaimed. "I wondered if our other guests would ever have the chance to meet you." She introduced the young man as Philip Warner, a visiting wildlife artist who had been staying with the Kaushiks for the past six months. He'd been up the coast for three days, studying some log-gerhead turtles there. He had an engaging manner, and Jody liked him immediately. So did Brittany, judging from the way she blushed when he shook her hand.

"So, you're all off to Mongla tomorrow, are you?" he inquired, having been filled in on the day's events. "It's market day, so you should have fun. Sadly, I can't join you — I'm heading into the forest to find a tiger."

"You won't have to go very far," said Brittany. "We just heard one outside." She tried to sound excited by the thought, rather than scared.

Philip's eyes brightened. "Great," he said. "On the doorstep!"

Just then, the phone rang, and Sunnu went to answer it. She was back five minutes later. "That was Mr. Vikram," she said, looking meaningfully at Shiv.

Shiv rolled his eyes at Jody.

"You must keep out of his way, Shivam," said his mother. "Please try not to return to that place."

Shiv looked as if he was about to protest, so Jody spoke up quickly. "So long as we see some dolphins on the river tomorrow, I won't mind if we don't go back to that island, Shiv. And hey — we've got a six-hour round trip river journey. We're bound to see dolphins, aren't we?"

May 26 — just before bed — Sukhi Rest House
Only ten hours to go before we head up the river to Mongla! I can't wait. It's going to be even more interesting now that nearly everyone has decided to come. Brittany was quite enthusiastic about the idea of a trip to Mongla since she heard that we might see some tigers from the safety of Dolphin Dreamer. *But then Ajay told her that tigers were very good swimmers. It took us ages to calm her down.*

There are so many exciting noises in the forest at night. The sounds come straight into our bedroom because our window faces into the trees. You can hear monkeys calling and strange grunts that may be the wild pigs they have around here. Brittany doesn't like any of the noises. She says they are scary. It's just as well she's fallen asleep already because I've just heard that tiger again, growling out in the forest. It sounded even closer than it did this afternoon. . . . Tigers don't climb in through first-floor windows, do they?

Jody leaned back from the *Dolphin Dreamer*'s deck rails and closed her eyes. The cool morning breeze in her hair felt wonderful.

They had left the Sukhi Rest House at seven that morning and had been chugging up the river for the last half hour. Harry was deliberately taking *Dolphin Dreamer* slowly, to avoid making the carburetor problem any worse.

Jody turned around when Shiv tapped her on the shoulder.

"Your father has been showing us his web site," he said in excitement. "I can't believe you can send all those pictures and stories to America."

"It's amazing, isn't it?" Jody agreed. "All my friends back in Florida log on to the web site to see where I am. Then they tell me in their e-mails how jealous they all are!"

Shiv peered over the side of the boat. "Have you seen any dolphins yet?"

37

Almost in answer to his question, the water broke about fifty yards ahead of the boat, and the sleek gray back of a dolphin emerged.

"Mom, Dad!" Jody called. "The dolphins are here!"

She watched closely as the water broke again. Was it an Irrawaddy? Could it even be the same one she and Shiv had seen the previous day, before they had met Mr. Vikram?

"It's a Susu," said Craig from behind her.

"Susie?" Jody echoed, confused. Since when did this dolphin have a name?

"No, not Susie!" Gina laughed, putting her arm around Jody's shoulders. "A Susu. It's another name for a Ganges River dolphin. This one is female, I think — she's quite large. Ganges River dolphins can grow up to about two and a half yards long if they're female, but males only get to just over two yards."

"Well, if she's female, we should call her Susie," said Jody promptly.

Susie the dolphin breached again. This time Jody could see a long, toothed beak poking above the water.

"Why does she hold her beak above the water like that?" she asked in fascination.

"Ganges River dolphins come up to breathe at a very sharp angle," Craig said. "A very visible beak is the result. Ganges River dolphins are naturally quite sociable, too."

Susie began a series of very fast clicks and whistles, nodding her strange, long beak in the air.

"She's definitely sociable," said Jody. "She's trying to talk to us!"

Jody leaned over the railing to get a closer look. Susie immediately spun over on one side and waved a flipper at Jody, who laughed and waved back.

"Actually, I think she's feeding." Gina smiled. "They use their flippers to sift through the mud on the riverbed, looking for food."

With one final cheerful whistle, Susie slipped below the churning surface of the river and was gone.

"She must have found something to eat," said Jody.

Craig nodded. "Maybe some tasty shrimp."

"Glad you've finally seen a dolphin," said Harry, stepping over to join them at the railing. Ravi and Sunnu followed him, talking quietly together. "I've seen one or two from the *Dolphin Dreamer* the past couple of nights."

"What else have you seen?" Jody asked.

"Crocodiles," said Harry promptly. "But you know that big one from the other day? Apparently, the fishermen haven't seen her since that morning. Maybe she's found some other fishermen to steal from."

Shiv looked surprised. "I have never known Chalaka to miss a day's fishing," he said.

Ravi and Sunnu also looked surprised, Jody thought. No, more than that — they looked concerned.

"When did the fishermen last see her?" Ravi asked.

"Like I told you," said Harry, "yesterday morning, at the catch."

Ravi and Sunnu exchanged a strange, silent glance. Jody was about to ask them what they were thinking, but her attention was caught by two or three birds — kingfishers, according to Dr. Taylor — that flew like lightning across the river. And then she forgot all about it.

The sun was already quite high in the sky when *Dolphin Dreamer* reached the town of Mongla. It felt like a different country from the peace and quiet of the Sukhi Rest House. Hundreds of people were milling along the riverbank, browsing at the market stalls that had been set up along the water. Boats of all shapes and sizes had docked at the long bamboo jetty, and Jody could hear lively Indian music floating across the water.

"Mongla likes to enjoy itself on market day," Ravi said to her as they all made their way up the jetty and into the town. "Making music and making money — they go together very well, don't you think?"

Harry checked his watch. "Cam and I will make our way to the boatyard," he said. "Ravi, can you show us where to go?"

"I suggest we all meet back at the boat in two hours," said Craig. "It'll give you all a chance to explore."

Mei Lin's eyes gleamed. "I'll enjoy putting together a banquet fit for a king from these." She laughed, indicating the market stalls. "Brittany, can you help me? We'll find some wonderful food, I'm sure."

Jody expected Brittany to say no. She didn't like

chores at the best of times. But Brittany looked excited at the prospect of shopping at all the different stalls and joined Mei Lin without a murmur.

"I don't envy the traders," remarked Gina as Mei Lin and Brittany headed into the heart of the market. "I think Mei Lin will drive a hard bargain!"

"Come on," said Shiv, grabbing Jody's hand and pulling her into the market. "Two hours isn't long for Mongla!"

Jody felt overwhelmed by the color and energy of the town as Shiv dragged her from place to place. There were piles of exotic fruit, bales of brightly colored cotton and silk, and squawking chickens and bleating goats everywhere. The air was warm and full of the smells of Sundarban life — animals and vegetables, burning incense, and muddy river water. Jody peered into stalls where men were having their hair cut, eating bowls of steamed fish, even having their teeth looked at by a market dentist. She saw stalls filled with wicker cages of tiny singing birds that filled the air with trilling and chirping. She even saw a monkey stealing a banana from a market stall before chattering

Busy Mongla market

and disappearing down the street at high speed, to the fury of the stallholder. Cheerful music pumped from every stall and every house along the way, and Jody lost all sense of time in the wonder of it all.

"Let's go and find Harry," said Shiv at last. "We must be back at the boat in a little while. Maybe he needs some help."

They wandered down a side alley to the river, where they found a large open-sided building on the waterfront. Boats in various stages of repair lay in front of it on the riverbank, and the inside of the building was filled with sounds of hammering and banging.

Jody peered around, trying to catch sight of Harry. Two men were talking at the far end of the boatyard. One of the men looked familiar — but it wasn't Harry.

"It's Mr. Vikram!" said Jody in surprise.

Shiv hissed through his teeth. "He will probably shout at us again if he sees us," he said. "I think we should stay back here for now."

They watched from a safe distance.

"He is talking to Khaled, the boatyard owner," Shiv explained for Jody's benefit.

"Mr. Vikram must be getting his boat fixed," said Jody.

Shiv frowned. "No, I think he is ordering a new boat. But maybe I heard wrong. Everyone knows Mr. Vikram has no money — his shellfish business is not doing so well at the moment."

They listened some more. Mr. Vikram was waving his hands and so was Khaled.

Shiv straightened up. "It's probably nothing." He shrugged. "Harry's not here, so let's go back to *Dolphin Dreamer.* I don't know about you, but I'm hungry."

"Good timing," Gina greeted them as they made their way down the bamboo jetty and boarded *Dolphin Dreamer.* "Mei Lin and Brittany have cooked up a feast, and we're about to dig in. How was your morning?"

Before Jody had a chance to reply, Jimmy gave a shout and pointed down the jetty. They turned to see Dr. Taylor staggering toward the boat, his arms absolutely full of fruit. A huge branch of papaya fruit hung over one shoulder and a branch of bananas over the other. He was doing his best not to drop the twenty or more mangoes he was balancing in front of him.

"Wretched traders . . . wouldn't take no . . . for an answer," he puffed as he reached the *Dolphin Dreamer.* "I didn't . . . want it, but they kept piling it on. Where's . . . Mei Lin? Maybe she can do something useful with all this."

He wobbled aboard and disappeared down into the galley.

"Well," Gina remarked in amusement, "thanks to Dr. Taylor, it looks like we're going to be enjoying some local fruits for the rest of our stay!"

May 27 — lunchtime — on deck, Mongla jetty
Everyone had a great time in Mongla this morning! Mom bought herself a gorgeous red-and-pink silk sari, and Sunnu has promised to show her how to put it on. The twins even got to see a snake charmer in the market. Khaled, the boatyard owner, came around to Dolphin Dreamer *and replaced the new carburetor himself in half an hour flat. The engine's now "purring like a tiger," as Harry puts it.*

On the subject of tigers, Brittany is sulking in her cabin because the twins and Ajay sneaked up behind her in the market and growled, making her scream and drop a bag of chapati flour she and Mei Lin had just bought. The bag burst and covered Brittany in flour from head to foot! Needless to say, Brittany didn't see the funny side, and she's still leaving a trail of flour whenever she moves around.

Shiv and I never got around to mentioning Mr. Vikram and the boatyard. He was probably there for a perfectly good reason, anyway. Must go, we're about to leave, and I want to make sure I get some of Dr. Taylor's fruit salad for dessert!

Jody forgot all about Mr. Vikram on the way back to the Sukhi Rest House. Susie, the Ganges River dolphin, bobbed up beside them again and did her best to keep the boat entertained for most of the journey. She was joined by several others, all waving their long beaks in the air for what looked like the sheer fun of it. But there was still no sign of an Irrawaddy dolphin. Jody was beginning to feel a little pessimistic.

The Sukhi Rest House was just coming into view when there was a shout from the bow.

"Irrawaddy!"

Jody's heart leaped in her chest. Had she heard Shiv right, or were her ears playing tricks on her?

Shiv was beckoning her, grinning. "Come over here, Jody!" he said. "Quickly, or you'll miss it!"

Jody flew to the far side of the boat, narrowly beating her parents and the others to a prime position by the railing. They all stared out into the river.

All that could be seen of the Irrawaddy dolphin was its neat, rounded head, as it sat up like a seal and stared at them from out of the water. Jody saw immediately how different this species of dolphin was from Susie. It had a thick flexible neck, and it seemed to be cocking its head as it looked at them. It didn't have the same smile as a bottle-nosed dolphin. Instead, its mouth was set in a straight line, giving it an air of dignity and wisdom. Jody noticed a small scar above one eye, which almost made the dolphin look as if it were raising one eyebrow.

"It's very calm, isn't it?" Jody whispered to Shiv as

she gazed into the small, deepset eyes of the little dolphin. "As if it knows the answer to world peace or something."

"Sandhi," said Shiv.

Jody turned around and looked at him, surprised. "What does that mean?" she asked.

"S-A-N-D-H-I," Shiv spelled it out. "It is a Hindi word. It means peace."

"I think that's what we should call her, then," said Jody.

"How do you know it's a she?" Gina laughed.

Jody smiled. "She just looks like a girl. Don't you think she's female?"

"More than likely," Craig admitted, "judging from her size."

Sandhi stared at them for a while longer with the grave wisdom of an owl. Then she turned her head slightly and looked directly at Jody. Jody wished desperately that she was a bit nearer. "Sandhi," she whispered again.

At last, the dolphin sank below the water, and Jody was left staring at the calm surface of the river.

4

Jody opened her eyes in the darkness of the night. It felt very late — perhaps one or two o'clock in the morning. Something she couldn't quite place had brought her out of a deep sleep.

"Jody?" came Brittany's scared voice. "Are you awake?"

Jody sat up and switched on the small bedside light.

Brittany was staring at her with large, frightened eyes. "I can hear the tiger," she whispered. "It sounds really close."

Jody heard a rumbling growl from the forest outside the window. Her heart hammered in her chest, but she stayed calm. "It's OK, Brittany," she said. "It's miles away. Go back to sleep."

Brittany frowned uncertainly then huddled down under her mosquito net. The tiger fell silent after a few more minutes. Soon Jody could hear Brittany breathing evenly, fast asleep again.

Jody switched off the light but lay awake for a while, listening to the noises of the night. Her mind was alert, and she didn't feel sleepy at all. The memory of Sandhi's serious dolphin face peeping out of the river earlier that day kept running through her head, making her smile. *Where did the little Irrawaddy come from?* she wondered. *Why hadn't they seen her before, if she lived close to the rest house?*

Jody decided that a drink of water might help her get back to sleep. She knew that the Kaushiks always kept a jug of ice water in the fridge, so she climbed quietly out of bed and made her way down to the kitchen.

At the bottom of the stairs, she stopped and listened. She could hear voices — Sunnu and Ravi were talking in the living room. Jody felt puzzled. It was very late.

What could they be talking about? From what she could hear, they sounded worried. Perhaps they were talking about the tiger?

She stood in the darkness for a moment, unsure what to do. Then she walked into the kitchen, filled a glass with cold water, and headed back up to bed. Whatever Sunnu and Ravi were talking about, it was none of her business.

Jody got up early the next morning and wandered outside to the jetty. Philip was painting, and he looked pleased to see her.

"What do you think?" he asked, indicating his painting. "It was over pretty quickly, but I think I got most of it down on canvas."

Jody settled down on the jetty beside him and looked around at the swirling morning mist that cloaked the river. "Weren't you worried about meeting the tiger face-to-face this morning?" she asked curiously. "Haven't you heard that expression yet, the one about 'Here the tiger is always watching you'?"

Philip shrugged. "You came out here, didn't you?"

"Yes," Jody said slowly, "but it was light already. You must have been out here in the dark."

"Well, between you and me, I wanted to see the tiger," Philip told her. "I like taking risks sometimes. It's just not the same, painting tigers from other people's photographs."

"You're pretty interested in tigers, aren't you?" Jody commented.

"Of course," Philip said. "You can't help being interested in tigers in this area. There are so many stories about them. Many people believe that they are magical spirits — wicked magicians or warriors! And because of these superstitions, in certain parts of the world tiger bones and other body parts are believed to have healing and strengthening powers. It makes them the most wonderful creatures to paint, knowing the myths that surround them."

"What else do you paint?" Jody asked.

"Loggerhead turtles," said Philip, ticking them off on his fingers. "Crocodiles. Rhesus monkeys, sometimes, and birds."

"Do you ever paint dolphins?" Jody asked eagerly.

"It has been known," said Philip, carefully putting his paints away in a battered leather case.

Before Jody could ask him any more questions, Philip stood up. "I'm going inside," he said. "Enjoy the rest of the dawn! But I have to say I'm dying for a cup of tea."

May 28 — early morning — on the jetty of the Sukhi Rest House
The tiger growled most of the night, and in between listening to it and thinking about Sandhi and Susie, my brain never got tired enough to go back to sleep. I thought I'd come out here and see if the fishermen were at work again, but I was too late — the sun had risen, and they'd brought in their catch already.

Philip Warner, the artist who's staying here, was sitting on the jetty beside Dolphin Dreamer *with his easel. He'd done a beautiful painting of the sunrise — bright slashes of pink and red. If I hadn't seen that amazing sunrise the other day, I would have thought he had made up the colors! Apparently, he didn't sleep very well last night, either. But his excuse was that he was too excited to sleep. He wanted to get outside and paint the tiger he could hear. I think he's only seen tigers from a distance, even though he's been here for more than six months. It must be very frustrating, trying to paint an animal that doesn't like the attention!*

Jody closed her diary and headed back into the rest house. Gina looked up from her cup of coffee as Jody entered the kitchen. "Morning." She yawned. "You and Philip are up early. Did you hear the tiger?"

"As if you could miss it," said Jody, sitting down. "Brittany woke up once, but then she slept like a rock through the rest of the night." She looked curiously at her mother. "Why are you up so early, Mom?" she asked.

Gina smiled. "I need to update the Dolphin Universe web site," she said. "Having seen that Irrawaddy yesterday, I now feel that I've got something to say. Web users haven't been logging on to hear about my new sari or how comfortable the beds in the Sukhi Rest House are."

"Did you get a picture?" asked Jody.

Gina shook her head. "Your dad and I left the camera here before we left for Mongla. I don't know what I'm going to do yet, but I'll think of something."

Philip had been drinking his tea, standing quietly beside the kitchen sink. Suddenly, he joined in the conversation. "I have a picture you could use," he said. "Not a photo, though, I'm afraid."

Gina looked at him with interest. "One of your paintings?" she asked.

"I have some sketches," he said modestly. "Just a few I've made recently. I'll show you, if you like. So long as your web users don't mind a bit of artistic license."

"How much license?" Jody queried.

Philip laughed. "I'm not into abstract art, if that's what you're wondering," he said. "Here, look." He rummaged in the large bag he was carrying and pulled out a sheaf of sketch paper, which he carefully spread out on the kitchen table.

Jody gasped. The pictures were beautiful. With a few bold pencil lines, Philip had captured several Irrawaddy dolphins perfectly. Their round heads, their solemn expressions, each dolphin had a separate and distinct character. One of the dolphins had a small scar above one eye. With mounting excitement, Jody felt sure that the picture was of Sandhi.

"These are wonderful, Philip," said Gina, staring intently at the pictures. "I'd love to use a couple. I think you may have just saved my life here. How much do we owe you?"

"Oh, I couldn't charge you," said Philip, embarrassed. "Just my name on the pictures will do."

"We'll make sure we give you a glowing review on the Dolphin Universe web page, then," said Gina, smiling. "Come on, let's go and scan these pictures in."

The scanner and computer were still on board *Dolphin Dreamer,* so Jody, Gina, and Philip made their way outside. The sun was rapidly burning off the morning mist, and the sky was getting brighter all the time.

"Philip," said Jody as Gina logged on to the web site and powered up the scanner, "where did you do those pictures? They are fantastic. I didn't know you could see so many Irrawaddies in one place."

Philip looked pleased. "A little bay I've found upriver," he said. "I don't think anyone else knows about it. A family of Irrawaddies lives there. I've been going there for a couple of months now. They used to disappear at the first sight of me, but they gradually got used to me. Now they genuinely don't seem to notice when I arrive."

"Can I ask where this place is?" asked Gina. "You see, Craig and I really need to collect some data on the Irrawaddy. We haven't had much luck so far. This family would be perfect research material for us."

Philip looked thoughtful. "I haven't taken anyone there before," he said. "Not even Shiv knows about it. I'm not sure the dolphins would appreciate a larger audience."

"I understand your concern, Philip." Gina nodded. "But I can't tell you how important our research is. The Irrawaddy's natural habitat is constantly under threat from development and pollution, and their numbers are dwindling. We really don't know very much about these little dolphins, and they need all the help they can get."

Philip was silent for a minute or two. "All right," he said

eventually. "I can see that it is important. And I hardly need to tell a dolphin expert about the need to respect these animals. I'll take you there later on, if you like."

Jody couldn't hold it in any longer. "Please can I come, too?" she begged. "I . . ."

She stopped. She couldn't put her finger on why it was so important to see the dolphins and possibly to see Sandhi again. She just knew with all her heart that all she wanted in the world was to see the Irrawaddy family in their secret home.

Philip shook his head. "I really don't think taking all three of you is a good idea," he said. "I'm sorry, Jody. We might drive them away from their home, and I'd hate to be responsible for that."

Jody's shoulders sagged. She could see Philip's point and respected him for making it. But it was very hard to hear.

Gina was looking thoughtful. "Jody is very good with dolphins, Philip," she said. "She's spent pretty much her whole life learning about them and living with them. I have a suggestion, which I hope you will consider."

Jody looked hopefully at her mother.

"How about if I drop out, and Jody takes my place?" Gina suggested.

"But, Mom, your research!" Jody gasped.

Gina smiled. "Philip, do you think I could go some other time?" she asked. "Craig can make notes on his own. I'd love to see the dolphins, but I think Jody might burst with frustration if we don't let her go. And she's got the makings of a great marine observer. What do you think?"

May 28 — afternoon — somewhere on cloud nine
I have the best mother in the world. I couldn't believe it when Philip agreed to take me instead of Mom to see the Irrawaddies. Dad was happy to have me along, so it's all set. We're going after lunch. I've never felt less like eating lunch in my life! I keep staring at my watch, wishing the hands would move faster. I might see Sandhi again this afternoon — up close!

"All set?" said Philip, grinning at Jody and her dad from behind the controls of the Kaushiks' small red launch.

Craig checked that he had everything he needed —

camera, notepad, pen. "As ready as I'll ever be!" He smiled, climbing into the launch.

Jody jumped aboard behind him. She had her camera with her and her diary. She knew they might end up waiting some time to see the dolphins, so she planned to describe every last detail of the secret bay in her journal.

The boat's engine gave a throaty roar, and Philip pulled away from the jetty. Soon they were speeding down the river, cutting through the breakers with ease. It was a good, powerful boat — unlike Shiv's little dinghy.

Philip took them off the main course of the river after about fifteen minutes. Soon the boat was cruising down smaller water channels, beneath a canopy of tall, dark mangrove trees. Left, right, left. He seemed to know his way very well.

At last, the launch drew up in a calm, leafy inlet. Philip moored the boat and motioned to Jody and Craig to step ashore. The island was quiet and serene, dappled with pale light filtering down through the trees.

Philip pointed to a shaded water channel just to the

left of a huge, gnarled tree. "The family bases itself here," he whispered, deftly setting up his painting stool and flipping open his sketchpad. "They aren't home yet, but they never stray very far. I expect they'll be along within the next hour or so. Are you OK waiting?"

Jody settled down beside the water. Her dad pulled out his notebook and camera and started jotting a few notes.

They waited for a while. In that time, Jody noticed all kinds of things about the Irrawaddies' inlet. Tiny red crabs appeared in the shoreline mud, waving bright red claws at the sky. Ropelike liana vines hung from the trees above them, thick and heavy. The brilliant flash of a butterfly caught Jody's eye, and she heard the distant chatter of a monkey somewhere up in the trees. She made a few notes in her diary and sketched some small dolphins in the margin.

At last, their patience was rewarded. Jody held her breath as three sleek gray bodies coasted silently into the inlet. One of the Irrawaddies promptly sank from view at the sight of visitors, but the other two seemed unconcerned.

Jody immediately recognized the smaller of the two

Our patience is rewarded. . . .

remaining dolphins. She'd know that face with its quizzical scar anywhere. Sandhi looked at her, tilting her rounded head just like a dog. Jody stared back happily.

Sandhi clicked rapidly at Jody, as if she was trying to communicate something. Then she flicked her tail and sank a few inches below the water until only her head was showing, still watching Jody with interest.

The third dolphin returned after about ten minutes,

apparently having decided that Jody and her father were harmless. Sandhi and her family stayed for another twenty minutes, feeding quietly along the riverbank. Jody thought of the little red crabs she'd seen earlier. They were obviously the Irrawaddies' favorite food.

Before long, the small family of dolphins turned on an unspoken command and headed back out to the river.

"I think that's it," said Philip regretfully, folding up his sketch pad. "Not long today, I'm afraid."

"It was a great start," said Craig with a smile. He capped his pen. "What beautiful animals. I got some lovely pictures. Thank you so much for bringing us, Philip."

Jody climbed into the launch and stared back over her shoulder as Philip pulled away from the shore. She hoped that Philip would bring her back someday soon. She felt her father's hand on her shoulder and looked around. Philip was pointing at something on the far shore.

Jody wasn't certain, but she thought she caught a glimpse of an orange-and-black-striped face, peering out at them from the undergrowth. Her whole body tensed. Was it a tiger? But within a moment, the face had vanished.

SNYDER COUNTY LIBRARIES, INC.
ONE NORTH HIGH STREET
SELINSGROVE, PA 17870

5

May 29 — evening — Sukhi Rest House
You wouldn't believe how much rain has fallen in the last twenty-four hours. I was relieved to wake up this morning and find that the rest house was still standing on the river-bank, not floating downstream. I had no idea that rain could be so noisy! It's been coming down all day, and it's pretty impressive to watch. The whole sky looks like a wa-terfall, and the river has been whipped up into a frothy, chocolaty swirl. Somehow, I don't think the fishermen went out this morning. Even Harry and Cam have been driven off Dolphin Dreamer and have been inside all day.

"I'm so *bored*," Brittany moaned, staring out the window. The rain was still falling steadily.

"But you've won the last five games!" objected Harry, staring down at the pack of cards he was holding in his hands. "How can you be bored?"

Jody put her cards down with a sigh. They had been playing most of the afternoon, and even she had to admit that it was getting pretty dull. She wondered how Sandhi and her family were doing. Did river dolphins suffer in bad weather like this? After all, they couldn't dive deep to escape the rain like sea dolphins.

"I hope it isn't the monsoon season already," said Ravi.

"So do I!" said Harry fervently. "After all that business with the carburetor, it would be really bad luck if the monsoons came early."

"We could be here for months." Jimmy sighed. "And we've played with all of Ajay's toys already."

Sunnu leaned over and whispered something to Ravi, who immediately frowned.

"Is something the matter?" asked Gina.

"I'm a little concerned . . ." said Sunnu, and then stopped.

"Concerned about what?" asked Jody, intrigued. She suddenly remembered the hushed conversation she'd overheard a couple of nights earlier. "Concerned about the tiger again?"

Craig snorted. "I think the tiger's probably too wet and miserable to be worrying about us," he said.

"No, not the tiger," said Sunnu slowly. "We think the tiger has left. We haven't heard it for a few days." She glanced at Ravi. "I'm just concerned about the roof," she said at last. "With all this rain, I think we may have a leak."

"I'll look at it for you tonight, Sunnu," Philip offered, looking up from his sketch pad. Jody was amused to see that he had been drawing her brothers and Ajay. He'd captured their bored faces perfectly.

"Thank you, Philip," said Sunnu, "but it really won't be necessary. Ravi has mended leaks in this roof before. It is very easy." She stood up. "Now I must prepare some supper for you. Please excuse me."

She walked into the kitchen. After a few moments, Ravi followed her. Jody was left with the strange feeling that they were still uneasy about something. And it wasn't the roof.

After supper, everyone made their excuses and went to bed early. There really was nothing else to do.

Brittany checked her bed suspiciously. "I bet the rain'll leak right onto my head in the night," she complained. "That would be typical."

Jody scrambled into bed and pulled the blanket up. "Brittany, do you think everything's OK with Ravi and Sunnu?" she asked.

Brittany looked surprised. "Apart from the leaking roof, you mean?" she queried. "Why wouldn't everything be OK?"

Jody shrugged. "I've just got a funny feeling," she said.

"So have I," Brittany grumbled, climbing into bed. "I've got a funny feeling about this leak. If I scream in the night, you'll know it's either the tiger or the leak that's got me." She suddenly grinned. "Maybe Philip would come and rescue me," she said coyly. "Don't you think he's gorgeous? Maybe it's worth screaming in the night just in case! 'Night, Jody."

Jody said good night and lay back in the dark, letting the sound of the drumming rain soothe her to sleep.

Brilliant sunshine was pouring into the bedroom when Jody opened her eyes the next morning. She jumped out of bed and ran to the window.

The Sundarbans looked magical. The leaves on the trees gleamed and shone in the sun. Wisps of steam rose from the wet, black trunks of the mangrove trees. The sky was a bright, glorious blue, and there wasn't a cloud in the sky. It was like a different place.

Brittany sat up in bed and yawned. "Sun at last!" she said sleepily. "It's about time."

Jody quickly pulled her clothes on and ran downstairs. Both her parents and Philip were already up and sitting around the table.

"It seems our fears about the monsoon were premature," said Gina with a smile, looking up as Jody came in. "Your father and I are going to take a look at the Ganges River dolphins today, Jody. Would you like to join us? Apparently, several families live about half an hour's walk downriver."

She looked across at Philip. "Alternatively," she said, "Philip is planning to head back to the Irrawaddy inlet for some more sketching. He says you were a pleasure to have along yesterday, and he wouldn't mind some more company today. Maybe you'd prefer to go back there?"

"What a choice!" Jody joked, helping herself to a bowl of cereal. "I'd love to see some more Ganges River dolphins again, Mom, but . . ."

"You've lost your heart to the Irrawaddies," Craig finished her sentence for her.

Jody flashed an apologetic smile at her parents. "You know me pretty well, don't you, Dad?" she said with a grin.

Normally, Jody would have jumped at the chance of spending the day with her parents to help them observe the Ganges River dolphins. But what her dad had said was true. There was something about the Irrawaddies, and Sandhi in particular, that had captured her imagination. She couldn't wait to see them again.

"That's fine," said Philip. "I think we may need to bring Shiv along as well, as all the rain has made the river a little trickier to navigate than the other day."

Brittany appeared in the kitchen. Jody noticed with interest that she'd applied a touch of makeup this morning and had taken particular care with her clothes.

"Morning, everyone," she said casually. She glanced across at Philip under her eyelashes. "Morning, Philip," she added, a blush creeping up her neck.

"And a gorgeous morning it is, too," said Philip, raising his mug of tea toward her.

Brittany blushed a little more and busied herself with cutting up a fresh mango.

Jody caught her mother's eye and tried not to laugh. It was so obvious that Brittany had a crush on Philip!

"So, what's everyone doing today?" Brittany asked, looking across at Philip again.

"This and that," said Craig.

"What about you, Philip?" Brittany looked hopefully across at the tall English artist.

"Jody and I are off sketching and admiring Irrawaddies," said Philip. "Shiv's coming, too, to help us navigate."

Brittany flicked her hair back from her face. "I love Irrabodies," she said earnestly. "Could I maybe come, too?"

"Are you any good at keeping quiet?" Philip asked, stirring his tea.

Jody managed to turn a laugh into a cough.

Brittany glared at her. "Oh, yes," she said, turning back to Philip. "So — could I come?"

"I don't see why not," Philip said after a moment. "The dolphins seemed fine with two visitors the other day. I think we might be able to risk three today. But we'll be leaving in about ten minutes. Think you'll be ready in time?"

Brittany had a mouthful of mango. She tried to nod eagerly, but somehow managed to choke and cough out the mango back onto her plate. Blushing fierily, she excused herself from the table and fled up to the bedroom.

Poor Philip, thought Jody with a grin. *What had he got himself into?* Twenty minutes later, Shiv eased the

Kaushiks' launch away from the jetty. The water was wild and frothy, and it was a struggle to get into the calmer water in the center of the river. Brittany shrieked and clutched Philip's arm — quite unnecessarily, Jody thought as she helped Shiv to hold the tiller still.

The sun blazed down on the water, which glared fiercely in the light. Through the rushing sound of the river, Jody could hear the steady *drip-drip-drip* of rain from the trees along the bank. It was as if the rainstorm had washed the whole of the Sundarbans clean.

"Are you sure it's this way?" said Jody, looking at the river with confusion. There were more channels than she remembered, and the river seemed much wider.

"Yes," said Philip, pointing at an enormous mangrove tree up ahead. "I always head for that tree over there. Then it's about another five minutes farther along, to the left."

Shiv obediently followed Philip's instructions, and the boat struggled along through the current. The river bubbled around them, flinging up waves and wetting them every now and again. Brittany's hair was looking frizzier by the minute, despite her surreptitious attempts to keep it smooth and close to her head. Jody tried not to think about the crocodiles, which she knew would happily gobble them all up if the boat overturned.

At last, Shiv drew the boat into the familiar inlet. The mossy green shore seemed smaller than it had before — the water levels had risen considerably in the night.

Brittany scrambled out of the boat. "So what do we do now?" she asked loudly.

"Shhh," said Philip, Jody, and Shiv immediately.

"Oops," Brittany whispered. "Sorry. So, what do we do?"

"We wait and see —" Philip began to say.

Jody touched his sleeve and pointed. The Irrawaddies were already skulling gently in the shallow water channel and feeding along the riverbed.

"I think they have been here for some time," Shiv whispered, settling down on the bank. "The storm has not disturbed the water here so much. They have been sheltering, I think."

Jody recognized Sandhi again with a rush of delight. The dolphin seemed pleased to see her — she kept her head boldly above the water and clicked softly in welcome. In the shallow inlet, Jody could see her more clearly. She had a stout middle, short powerful flippers, and a small dorsal fin on her back.

The other two dolphins still kept their distance, although Jody could see their markings this time. She guessed they were both male. The bigger one had a nick in his dorsal fin, and the other had a mottled marking on his flank.

"They're cute," said Brittany, sounding as if she didn't really care. She yawned and checked her watch. "How long are we staying?"

"Just until I get that smaller male down on paper," said Philip, busily sketching. "He's pretty elusive. This is the first time he's stayed still long enough for me to draw him."

Brittany moved closer to the water. "Hey, this one's letting me get really close!" she said, forgetting to keep her voice down. "I think he likes me!"

The big male lay stock-still in the water, watching

Brittany with beady black eyes as she approached. Suddenly, the dolphin's muscular back flexed, and he squirted her sharply with a jet of water.

"Hey!" Brittany jumped up with a bellow.

The others burst out laughing. Even the dolphins, who had retreated away from the shore, seemed to be grinning.

"He didn't like you so close!" spluttered Shiv.

Brittany gets a surprise!

"That was amazing!" said Jody. "I've never seen a dolphin spit water like that before."

"Well, I hope I never see it again," said Brittany furiously, mopping herself up. "Now look at me!"

There was a sudden crashing sound in the undergrowth. Something was approaching them fast.

"What's that noise?" Brittany quavered, looking fearfully into the dark green forest.

"Quick," said Shiv instantly. "Into the boat!"

He hustled them toward the launch, looking over his shoulder the whole time. The rustling was getting louder. Jody's stomach lurched. What if it was a tiger?

"What —" she began as she jumped into the boat, pulling Brittany in after her.

"No time to argue!" Shiv insisted, pushing Philip into the boat and leaping in behind him. "It's a boar!"

An ugly-looking wild pig shot out of the undergrowth, snorting furiously. Its legs pounded like pistons, and it cut a huge swath through the grass and bamboo. Brittany shrieked. In a few whirlwind seconds, the boar disappeared again, plowing a long, pale furrow through the jungle and out of sight. A line of small, heavy hoofprints showed that it had charged straight across the area where they had all been sitting only moments before.

"Well," said Shiv after a moment of silence, "he was in a hurry." He looked very serious for a moment. "I think maybe a tiger was after him."

Brittany looked even more panic stricken. "I don't want to be eaten by a t-tiger!" she wailed.

Jody tried to breathe normally, but her chest felt as if it were about to explode. Her legs felt loose and wobbly, like two pieces of string. Boars didn't get out of the way for just anybody. She'd seen the animal's sharp tusks and the way they cut through the grass like butter.

"Is everyone OK?" asked Philip.

Brittany let out a sob, and he put his arm around her. Jody looked across the bow of the boat to the Irrawaddy inlet. She wasn't surprised to see that the dolphins had disappeared.

"I think we should stay in the boat for a few more minutes," Shiv suggested. "Then we can go back. The boar won't return. And it wasn't really being chased by a tiger, Brittany," he added, looking slightly shamefaced. "I was only joking. Boars do that all the time."

"Some joke." Brittany sniffed and huddled up to Philip again.

"The dolphins may not come back today," said Philip, "but I'd like to wait a little longer, just in case."

Jody looked back at the path the boar had carved through the forest. It looked like a neat, inviting tunnel. "I'd like to check that out," she said suddenly, pointing at the tunnel. "See where it goes. Do you think it's safe, Shiv?"

Shiv smiled. "We will wait a little while, just to make sure the boar has gone," he said. "Then we can go, if we are careful. Maybe we'll find some more animals I can tell you about."

"I'll stay with Philip," said Brittany immediately.

They waited ten minutes more, just to make sure that the boar wasn't coming back. Then, cautiously, they climbed ashore again.

"We'll be back in fifteen minutes," Jody promised as she and Shiv headed down the boar's path.

"OK," said Philip, settling down beside the water again with Brittany beside him. "No rush."

Picking her way through the grass, following Shiv into the forest, Jody felt a shudder of fear. The forest was such a strange place. Maybe this wasn't such a good idea. But somehow, she knew she was safe with Shiv. She trusted him not to let them come to any harm.

The forest grew darker. The boar's path plowed ahead of them, straight as an arrow. Jody looked up. The tops of the trees disappeared above her, straight and tall. Birds screeched among the leaves, and she heard quiet rustling in the grass and roots at her feet. The forest had a magical quality about it. Jody felt she could walk forever and never reach the end.

"Hey!" Shiv exclaimed, bringing Jody up short where the boar's path ended at a deep water channel. "Look at that!"

Jody looked, but didn't quite believe what her eyes were telling her. If the boar hadn't ripped away part of the undergrowth, they would never have seen it. A gleaming speedboat was lying in front of them, bobbing gently in the water.

6

"What a beautiful boat," Jody remarked, staring at it. She couldn't help wondering why someone would leave it lying around in the middle of the forest. It didn't look like the kind of boat the fishermen used, but they hadn't seen any tourists around.

"Yes, it is beautiful," Shiv agreed with a frown. "But why is it here?"

The smell of fresh paint wafted up to them. The boat was sleek and fast looking. It had no name, just a serial number painted on its side. A canvas tarpaulin covered the open seats. Jody pulled it back and sniffed at the combination of fresh engine oil and new leather seats. Nothing had been left in the boat. It looked as if it had never been used. But if that were true, what was it doing here in the middle of nowhere?

Jody looked around, but there was no sign of anyone. It was just her and Shiv, standing in the dappled green silence of the mangrove trees.

"I think we should show Philip," said Shiv, looking at her.

Without waiting for Jody's reply, he turned around and started back toward Philip and Brittany. Jody hurried after him, her head full of questions.

"That was quick," said Philip, looking up from his sketch pad as they burst out of the undergrowth.

Jody noticed immediately that Sandhi and her family had returned. They were gliding together in the shallows and feeding along the bottom of the river again, as if the boar had never been there.

"We found something strange," Shiv blurted out.

Brittany looked scared. "The boar isn't heading back this way, is he?"

"We found a boat hidden in the undergrowth," said Jody. "We think you should see it, too."

Philip stood up. "A boat?" he echoed curiously. "But no one ever comes here! I should know, I've been here often enough. Where is it?"

Shiv led the way back down the boar's tunnel. Jody was next, followed closely by Philip and Brittany. This time, Jody didn't notice the light, or the silence, or the animal noises that were coming from every side.

Brittany, on the other hand, did. "It's pretty dark in here," she said anxiously. "Are you sure this is OK?" She shrieked as a monkey above her gave a loud scream that echoed around the trees.

"It's just a little farther," said Jody over her shoulder.

"But what if there are snakes?" Brittany whimpered.

Philip reached out and took her hand. "No snakes are going to get you," he said reassuringly.

Brittany blushed. Then she gave a wobbly smile and fell silent. Jody decided that Philip was a very useful influence on Brittany's theatrical nerves.

Shiv came to an abrupt stop at the end of the path. "There," he said, pointing.

The boat was still bobbing gently in the water channel in front of them.

Philip whistled. "That's some machine," he said admiringly. "But what on earth is it doing here?"

"That's what we want to know," Jody agreed, frowning.

The river was just as swollen and full on the way back. But this time, Shiv was taking the Kaushiks' launch with the flow of the water. It flew along like an arrow, sometimes dangerously fast, spinning and swirling on the changing currents. Shiv had a difficult time controlling the tiller, even with Jody's help. They all got soaked, and narrowly avoided crashing into the shore once or twice.

At last, Shiv pulled the launch safely out of the fast-running currents in the middle of the river and guided it into the Sukhi Rest House jetty.

Harry Pierce had been watching them approach from the deck of *Dolphin Dreamer.* Jody noticed that he and Cameron had lashed down the sails as tightly as they would go. Harry clearly wasn't taking any chances with the weather.

When they got close to the jetty, Harry jumped off *Dolphin Dreamer* and strode toward them, beckoning for the rope. Shiv lobbed it upward. It went whistling toward Harry with perfect accuracy.

"You're a handy sailor, Shiv," Harry said admiringly, lashing the rope firmly to the jetty. "That looked like a tough trip."

Tough is an understatement, Jody thought. She'd never been so pleased to see solid ground in her life.

"More of a roller-coaster ride," Brittany joked nervously, climbing onto the jetty.

Philip passed his bag and his stool up to Brittany and climbed out of the boat as well. "I have to say, I've enjoyed roller-coaster rides more," he confessed. "You know that they don't have crocodiles waiting for you if you fall out!"

"Come on," Shiv said urgently, scrambling onto the jetty. "Let's go and tell the others about that boat we found. My parents will want to know."

"Careful!" Jody called after him as he ran toward the rest house. "The jetty is very slippery — oh!"

She watched in horror as Shiv suddenly lost his footing in a smooth, shining puddle of water. He skidded sharply, flew up in the air, and then landed on the deck with a sickening crunch. He lay ominously still.

"Shiv!" screamed Brittany, rushing up to him. "Are you OK?"

"Philip, go and get the Kaushiks," said Harry urgently, running down the jetty.

"Right away," Philip said, and sprinted toward the house, calling for Sunnu and Ravi.

Shiv takes a tumble!

87

Jody flew toward her friend, her heart hammering in her chest. To her enormous relief, Shiv groaned and opened his eyes.

"My ankle . . . hurts," he said through gritted teeth.

Jody could see that his left ankle was already swelling up.

"Just lie still," said Harry. "Your parents will be out in a minute."

The Kaushiks ran out on the deck, followed closely by Philip and the McGraths.

"What happened?" Gina exclaimed.

"Shiv ran and slipped," Jody explained, pointing at the offending puddle.

Jimmy and Sean peered down at Shiv, who was lying on his back, groaning quietly. "Cool," said Jimmy, impressed. "Look, his ankle looks like a balloon. Do you think maybe it's broken?"

"Did it go *snap*?" Sean asked Brittany.

Brittany was taking off her jacket to put under Shiv's head. "What a disgusting question," she complained.

Ajay pushed forward. "That's nothing," he said. "I broke both my ankles once."

"Not at the same time, Ajay," said Ravi wryly.

Sunnu felt Shiv's ankle, and Shiv moaned with pain. "I don't think it's broken," she said at last.

"Shouldn't we get a doctor?" Craig asked with concern.

"The nearest doctor is fifty miles away," said Ravi. "We only call him in an emergency. Sunnu has a medicine kit. We will have him as good as new before you know it."

Sunnu gently wrapped up Shiv's ankle with a bandage she had brought out of the house. Then Philip and Craig helped him to his feet.

"I think we'll put you in bed and give you something to help you sleep," said Sunnu, stroking Shiv's forehead gently. "Sleep is the best thing."

Philip lifted Shiv up and carried him into the house. *It must hurt a lot if Shiv isn't complaining about going to bed,* Jody thought. She knew that he hated sitting still or sleeping any longer than he had to.

Philip and Craig helped Shiv up to bed.

"Come with me, Jody." Sunnu beckoned her into the kitchen.

Jody followed and watched as Sunnu set to work in the kitchen, pulling leaves and seeds out of a small box she kept by the sink. Sunnu pounded them together with a handful of cornmeal and a splash of water. The result was a gluey brown paste with a sharp antiseptic smell.

"What are you going to do with that?" Jody asked.

"I'll put this on his ankle," Sunnu said. "It will help the healing."

"But what is it?" Jody wanted to know.

Sunnu smiled. "A forest remedy," she said. "The Sundarbans is like a giant medicine kit, if you know where to look for plants." She rinsed out the bowl and took a handful of different leaves. She pounded them together, as she had with the poultice for Shiv's ankle. Only this time, she added hot water and sugar and poured the concoction into a mug.

"Here," she said, handing the mug to Jody. "Can you take it up to Shivam? He will be glad of it."

Jody sniffed it. A warm, lemony scent rose from the mug. It smelled nice, and Jody hoped it would work. It was certainly very different from any of the medicines her doctor had prescribed for her back home!

Shiv had taken three sips before falling asleep, his forehead less creased with pain now. As she slowly came back downstairs, Jody was filled with a new respect for the Sundarbans, its magical plants, and the wisdom of its people.

She yawned hard as she walked into the kitchen. Although it was barely four o'clock, she felt exhausted. It had been a very long day.

"Come and sit down," said Gina, patting the stool next to her in the kitchen. "You look wiped out. Did those Irrawaddy dolphins give you the runaround today?"

Jody sank down next to her mother. "No, they were lovely," she said. "But then a boar came and we had to jump into the boat —"

Suddenly, she remembered the boat in the inlet. With all the excitement about Shiv, it had totally gone out of her head. Quickly, she told the others.

"A speedboat?" exclaimed Ravi, leaning forward at the table. "Are you sure?"

"It was brand-new, and we think someone had hidden it," said Jody. "If the boar hadn't run through the undergrowth, we would never have seen it."

"This is serious," said Ravi. There was a new heaviness in his voice. "It means that our suspicions may be right." He glanced at Sunnu.

"What suspicions?" Craig asked with surprise.

"Poachers," said Sunnu quietly.

There was a sudden shocked silence.

"Ravi and I have believed for some time that something was wrong in the forest," Sunnu continued. "We heard stories of animals disappearing."

"That old crocodile!" said Brittany suddenly.

Sunnu nodded. "Also some turtles a week before you came. We heard about them on the UNESCO radio band. Marine turtles are rare, and UNESCO watches them closely. And we are now wondering about the tiger we have heard lately. All of a sudden, it has been very quiet."

"That's why you were worried the other day!" Jody exclaimed, putting two and two together as she recalled the voices she had overheard in the night and the strange conversation about the leaking roof.

Ravi nodded apologetically. "We didn't want to worry you until we had some kind of proof. The leaking roof was also a concern, but it is true — the poachers were worrying us more."

"This is not the first time, I'm afraid." Sunnu sighed. "They came six months ago." She looked at Jody. "You know the Irrawaddy dolphin family you have been visiting? There are only three of them, yes?"

Jody nodded with dread in her heart.

"Six months ago, there were five," said Sunnu simply.

Jody gasped. Sandhi had lost two members of her family to poachers? It didn't seem possible. "But why do the poachers want Irrawaddy dolphins?" she asked. "They're hardly ever kept in captivity. They aren't natural performers. Surely poachers would take bottlenosed dolphins or other more sociable species. I don't understand."

Gina took Jody's hand. "They are not taken for zoos, Jody," she said as gently as she could.

"Your mother is right," Ravi said. "There is a rich trade in the Far East for dolphin meat and oil. Places like China and Japan. The meat is smuggled over the borders. The smugglers bribe the customs officers, and it is hushed up. It is an ugly business."

It took a moment for Ravi's words to sink in. Jody put her hand to her mouth. She felt sick.

"Tiger bones, too," Ravi continued. "And crocodiles and turtles. It is said that these animals have powerful spirits, and, if you use them in medicines, they can work miracles."

Jody remembered the conversation she had had with Philip on the jetty a couple of days earlier, about tigers and their magical qualities. Hearing about the poachers gave Philip's stories a sinister meaning.

"But that's not true!" Jody burst out.

"We know," said Sunnu sadly. "Also, I think the poachers know. But they can make a lot of money this way, and so they do not care."

Visions of Sandhi and the rest of her family being

taken by the poachers filled Jody's mind. "We have to stop them," she said passionately. "Before they kill any more animals. Now that we've found their boat, surely we can stop them?"

"We don't know for sure that the boat belongs to the poachers," Philip pointed out.

"But we can start inquiring, can't we, Ravi?" asked Craig.

Ravi nodded. "We will also tell the UNESCO officials. They are very worried about preserving the forest from men like these poachers, and they have special means to help us — boats and trained men. They work closely with the police, too." He looked very solemn. "If we are right and the poachers are back, we will need all the help we can get."

Something was stuck in Jody's mind — something about a new boat. She had a feeling it might be very important. "I want to go back to the inlet," she said, standing up abruptly from the table. "I think maybe I know something about the boat."

The others looked at her in surprise.

"Maybe?" said Brittany, raising her eyebrows.

"That's the thing," said Jody, irritated with herself. "I can't remember exactly what. If I see the boat again, maybe I'll remember."

And maybe I won't, she thought unhappily. *But I've got to try.*

7

Craig checked his watch. "We have enough time before dusk begins to fall," he said. "And the river looks calmer. Jody, do you really think returning to the inlet will help you to remember something useful?"

"I'm not sure, Dad," Jody confessed. "But I think we should go, anyway. I want to see if the dolphins are OK." That was her biggest fear — that Sandhi and her family might be spirited away by the poachers before they returned.

"I haven't seen these dolphins yet," said Gina, stand-

ing up from the table. "I'll come with you. Ravi, Sunnu —
do you want to join us?"

Ravi shook his head. "I have to stay here," he said. "I
will make some phone calls and start asking about the
boat. I'll also contact UNESCO."

"I must stay for Shiv," said Sunnu, "and the other children, too. Also, your friends aren't back from their trip
yet. I should be here when they return."

Dr. Taylor, Maddie, Cam, and Mei Lin had gone on a
tour that morning, traveling with a group of honey collectors deep into the forest. The collectors only
worked in April and May, and they covered parts of the
Sundarbans that very few people had ever seen.

Ravi frowned. "The river is very difficult to navigate
after the heavy rain," he said. "The waters are a little
calmer now, but I am concerned that you may have dif-
ficulty reaching the inlet again."

"I'll go with them," Philip offered immediately. "I've
been taking the boat there for several months, and I
know the route. And after Shiv's help this morning, I
think I know what to do now that the river is so high."

"I don't want to go again," said Brittany decisively.

"That boat ride today made me feel sick. I can get rides like that at the fairgrounds back home."

"That's good." Sunnu smiled. "You can help me to prepare supper and keep an eye on Shivam and the other children."

Sean, Jimmy, and Ajay were tumbling around the living room, laughing and joking. Little Ambika was watching them with wide, dark eyes.

"We'll be back as soon as we can," Craig promised the Kaushiks. "And, hopefully, Jody will have remembered something useful about this mysterious boat. We'll do everything in our power to help you stop these poachers, don't worry."

The Kaushiks still looked anxious as they waved Jody, her parents, and Philip off at the jetty. And with good reason — the river was still high and whirled around the boat as Philip steered them back up the river.

Fortunately, the river seemed a little easier to navigate this time. The waters were beginning to calm down again after the rain, and they reached the inlet after less than half an hour.

Jody jumped ashore and lashed the boat to the mangrove tree stump, as before. She ran to the far side of the island — but the water channel was silent and empty.

"They aren't here," she said as her parents joined her at the water's edge. "I hope . . ." She left the sentence unfinished. She knew her parents understood her perfectly.

"I'm sure they're safe, Jody," Craig said gently. "After all, you've been here before when they haven't been around. And they'll be even safer once we've sorted out the mystery with this boat. Now, where is it?"

The boar's trail was still clearly marked as Jody led her parents through the forest. They found the boat again within five minutes. Craig looked it over carefully, peering under the tarpaulin and running his hand along the sleek painted hull.

"Well?" Gina prompted, looking hopefully at Jody. "Does it ring any bells, now that you've seen it again?"

Jody stood and stared at the boat. Images swam up inside her mind — a conversation she had heard recently. But the details stayed firmly out of reach. "I'm sorry," she said with frustration. "Nothing."

Chewing her lip, she followed her parents back down the boar's trail, looking back over her shoulder a couple of times. But the boat was keeping its secret locked up tight.

"The dolphins are back!"

Philip's exclamation brought Jody speedily back to reality. She ran eagerly over to the water's edge with her parents.

"Two males!" Gina said with satisfaction. "Aren't they beautiful?"

Only two? Jody looked. Sure enough, the mottled male and the big one that had spat water at Brittany were clearly visible in the shallow water. Where was the female? Where was Sandhi?

"Sandhi's missing," she burst out, falling to her knees and looking desperately up and down the water channel. "The female, the one I've been watching."

Gina and Craig looked at each other with concern.

"Does she always stay with the males?" Craig asked.

Jody tried to think. "The first time we saw her in the river, she was alone," she said. "But every time we've been to the inlet, they have been together."

"It's true," Philip agreed, looking concerned. "Either we have seen all three of them here, or none at all."

Jody wanted to block her ears and pretend she wasn't listening. But the facts were staring her in the face. There were poachers in the forest, and Sandhi was nowhere to be seen.

May 30 — early evening — at the Irrawaddy inlet
We've been waiting here for an hour, in case Sandhi comes back. Dad's worried about the poachers returning, but Mom and I wanted to stay as long as we could. The two males don't look worried, and there is no sign of a struggle along the riverbank, so those are good signs, I guess. Also, the boat doesn't seem to have moved since we were last here. But I can't help thinking that maybe Sandhi has been snatched, caught out in the middle of the river or something. Oh, where is she? Why isn't she here?

Everyone was silent and worried as Philip steered the boat back out into the center of the river. Night was falling, and it was important that they get back before the sun set and it was too dark to navigate.

Jody's mind was so full of worry for Sandhi and frustration at not being able to remember whatever it was that was bothering her about the boat, that she didn't notice which route they were taking back to the rest house. Gradually, she realized that they were moving along a stretch of river she'd never seen before. With a sudden sense of unease, she remembered the breathtaking ride they'd had that morning and how fast they had gotten home.

"Philip," she asked hesitantly, "shouldn't we be back by now? Are you sure we're going the right way?"

Craig and Gina stopped their conversation and looked up in alarm.

Philip was frowning and studying the water. "I think this is right," he said doubtfully. "We've passed the big mangrove tree that I usually steer by. Maybe the water just looks different. It's hard to tell after all the rain."

Jody looked again. She was sure she would have remembered the tangled roots of a mangrove tree jutting out of the riverbank to her left. The roots snaked up out of the water in a big loop, causing little currents to jump and swirl around them. "I've never seen those roots before," she said.

Philip looked. "Maybe they've appeared because of the rain," he suggested. "The landscape changes all the time in this forest, Jody."

"But the water levels have been rising, haven't they?" Jody persisted. "And if they've been rising, surely any roots would be hidden by water, not revealed?"

There was no denying the logic of Jody's argument. They were lost.

Suddenly, Jody noticed a crop of tall, straight bamboo on the riverbank to her left. It looked familiar. "Over there." She pointed. "I'm sure that's the right way."

"Do you think we should land and think about this?" asked Gina, peering over the edge of the boat. "We don't want to disappear into the forest forever."

Philip steered the boat toward the bamboo and threw the rope over the stump of a mangrove tree at the water's edge. "Now, we passed the large mangrove tree about ten minutes ago," he began.

The bamboo rustled. Everyone jumped as a man suddenly appeared out of the undergrowth. With a sinking feeling, Jody recognized him. It was Mr. Vikram.

"You again!" he shouted, shaking his fist at Jody. "Didn't I tell you to go away from here and not come back?"

Craig put his hands in the air, confused. "Excuse me, do we know you?"

Mr. Vikram took a step toward the boat. Jody shrank back against the wooden seat.

Mr. Vikram isn't pleased to see us. . . .

"You are trespassing!" Mr. Vikram yelled. "Go, and don't come back!"

"Are you Mr. Vikram?" asked Gina suddenly. "We're lost, you see, and —"

Mr. Vikram wasn't listening. He kept looking over his shoulder, back into the bamboo. Halfway through Gina's explanation, he turned back toward her and spoke loudly and furiously in Hindi.

"Mom, he won't listen," said Jody, tugging at Gina's sleeve. "Come on, let's go. I think maybe I can find my way back from here — I came here with Shiv the other day, remember?"

"Yes, go!" Mr. Vikram said rudely. "And don't come back!" He turned and disappeared into the bamboo.

"Well," said Gina, helping Philip to untie the rope. "That must be the rudest man I've ever met."

"Remember, his wife died last year," Craig reminded her as the boat pulled out into the middle of the river again. "We shouldn't judge him too harshly."

"Maybe, but I don't think that's any excuse for behaving like that," said Gina.

Jody stood with Philip at the helm of the boat and

helped him to steer in the direction she thought the rest house was. But something was wrong. She had a horrible feeling that they were still lost.

The sun was sinking rapidly, and the water blazed with red and orange reflections. Logs and pieces of wood torn from the trees in the storm floated past, making Jody think of crocodiles. She tried not to think about what might happen if they still hadn't found the rest house in half an hour.

There was a sudden familiar cacophony of whistling and clicking off the back of the boat.

"It's Susie!" Forgetting the danger for a moment, Jody scrambled eagerly to the back of the boat.

Susie, the long-beaked Ganges River dolphin, nodded and clicked at them, beating her tail from side to side and swimming smoothly up beside the boat. She dived and rolled and came back up for air, holding her beak straight out of the water.

"Did you know that Ganges River dolphins are effectively blind underwater?" Gina told Jody. "They find their way around using echolocation — vocalizing and measuring the echoes to judge the distance."

"I wish this one would use its echolocation skills to get us home," said Craig ruefully. "I don't mean to scare you, Gina, but we still don't know where we are, and it's getting darker every minute."

Susie swam off a little way before turning back again toward the boat. She did this several times, clicking more and more urgently.

"I think she wants us to follow her," suggested Jody with a surge of hope.

"That only happens in movies, Jody," said Philip. "Not in real life."

"Let's follow her, anyway," Jody said persistently. "She's going in more or less the direction we are. And she knows where we're staying, doesn't she?"

With a skeptical sigh, Philip steered the boat to the left and followed the dolphin.

"It does seem a little unlikely," Craig began as the boat rounded a bend into a wider part of the river.

But Jody gave a triumphant shout. "Look! *Dolphin Dreamer!*" *Thank you, Susie,* she thought fervently.

Craig and Gina sighed with relief to see the familiar shape of *Dolphin Dreamer* silhouetted against the sunset and bobbing gently at its mooring by the Sukhi Rest House jetty. They were home!

Philip raised his hands in the air with a laugh. "OK, dolphins can navigate!" he said cheerfully. "I'll never underestimate them again."

Susie surfaced beside the boat again and whistled loudly. Then she turned on her side and swam off to the left, away from the boat.

"Look, she's waving." Craig grinned as they watched her go, one flipper trailing above the water.

It certainly seemed that way. Susie gave a final volley of clicks and sank from view.

8

May 31 — almost bedtime — Sukhi Rest House
I wish I felt happier. It was a miracle that we found the
rest house after getting so lost, and it was fantastic to see
Susie again, but now that we're back, all I can think of is
Sandhi and where she might be. Maybe she's in a cage
somewhere, or maybe she's already . . .

Jody snapped her diary shut with a determined shake
of her head. She wouldn't give up hope, not yet.
They didn't have any proof that Sandhi had been
stolen.

The last rays of sun had faded from the sky almost as soon as they had landed at the Sukhi Rest House jetty. Ravi and Sunnu had come running out to meet them, and Jody felt an overwhelming sense of relief to see their welcoming faces. Sunnu then cooked everyone a large meal, and they all swapped stories with Dr. Taylor, Maddie, Mei Lin, and Cam, who'd had a very interesting day with the local honey collectors. But soon after the meal, Jody felt her spirits sinking as she thought about Sandhi and had come up to her room for some peace and quiet as soon as she could.

Suddenly, Jody really wanted to talk to Shiv. He would understand how she was feeling. Putting her diary on the bedside table, she padded down the hall to Shiv's room. The curtains were shut, and a fan whirred gently in the darkness.

"Jody?" Shiv said sleepily. "Is that you?"

"Good, you're awake!" Jody hurried over to him in relief. "How are you feeling?"

Shiv switched on the light beside his bed and yawned. "A little better," he said, rubbing his head. "My ankle still hurts, and I think I got a bang on my head as well. But my mother knows how to treat a sprained ankle. I will be walking again tomorrow, I hope."

They both looked down at Shiv's ankle, which had been tightly bound in neat cream-colored bandages.

"What have I missed?" Shiv asked. "What did everyone say about the boat?"

Jody explained what had happened since Shiv's accident and how the Kaushiks had told them about the poachers. She also described the return to the Irrawaddy inlet and how Sandhi was missing.

"Then we got lost coming back, and to top it off, we bumped into Mr. Vikram again," she said. "He was just as angry as before, of course."

"Did you tell the others that we saw Mr. Vikram in Mongla the other day at the boatyard?" said Shiv, suddenly alert.

Jody smacked her forehead with her hand. "Of course! *That's* what's been bugging me!" she exclaimed. "Something's been bothering me about the boat, Shiv — I felt like I knew something important, but I couldn't remember what. How could I have forgotten? We saw Mr. Vikram in Mongla, buying a new boat! The boat at the inlet — it must be his!"

They stared at each other as this information sank in.

"Does that mean that Mr. Vikram . . . is a poacher?" Jody said at last.

Shiv frowned. "I don't think so," he said. "He is a strange man, but he is not a bad one. He's just un-happy."

"But how do you explain that conversation we over-heard at the boatyard?" Jody persisted.

"I don't know," Shiv admitted. "Maybe I didn't hear it right. Let's go down and tell the others, anyway."

He started to get up, but Jody stopped him. "You shouldn't get out of bed."

"I'm OK," Shiv insisted. He swung his legs over the edge of the bed, tested his foot on the ground, and winced.

Jody reached forward. "Here, lean on me," she sug-gested.

Shiv draped one arm gratefully around Jody's shoul-ders and hopped a few steps. "That's fine," he said.

"Come on, let's go downstairs. My parents can make a phone call to Khaled at the Mongla boatyard. He will know for sure if Mr. Vikram was buying a boat."

Very slowly, Jody and Shiv made their way downstairs. Jody was bursting to move faster, but she carefully helped Shiv down each step.

Jody's brothers and Shiv's brother and sister were all asleep already, but the others were all gathered in the living room as they came in.

"Shiv, you should not be out of bed!" Sunnu exclaimed, jumping to her feet.

"We've remembered about the boat," said Jody, helping Shiv into a chair and sitting down beside him. "We think it belongs to Mr. Vikram."

Now she had the whole room's attention. She explained everything as quickly and clearly as she could.

When she had finished, Craig whistled. "It certainly looks strange," he said. "Ravi, what do you think?"

Ravi stood up. "I'm going to call the boatyard in Mongla," he said.

"Isn't it a little late?" said Dr. Taylor doubtfully.

"Khaled lives at the boatyard," Sunnu explained. "He will be at home now, I'm sure."

"If the boat really is Mr. Vikram's," said Jody, "do you think that proves he is a poacher?"

"No," Ravi replied. "It will simply prove that he is the owner. But it is a start. Now, can you describe the boat for me, Jody?"

Jody explained the shape and size of the boat as best as she could. Craig and Gina added the color of the leather seats and the tarpaulin. Best of all, Shiv came up with the serial number they had seen on the side of the boat.

"How did you remember the number?" Brittany asked in amazement as Ravi went to make the call.

Shiv shrugged. "It was easy," he said. "When you live with boats like we do, you remember things like that."

They waited in silence. Jody tried to listen at first, but Ravi was speaking Hindi. She glanced at Shiv's expression, but he wasn't giving anything away.

At last, Ravi came back into the room. "Khaled has certainly seen Mr. Vikram recently," he confirmed, looking around at everyone. "Mr. Vikram has just bought a new boat. With cash. He made the final payment and took the boat away with him the same day that we were in Mongla. And the serial number matches the one you gave me, Shiv."

"I knew it!" said Jody triumphantly.

"This only proves that he bought the boat," Gina cautioned.

"But it's a start, as Ravi said," Jody pointed out. "Now we just need to speak to Mr. Vikram."

Ravi and Sunnu looked at each other.

"That is easier said than done," said Ravi. "Remember, he is not a very friendly neighbor."

"I've got it!" said Shiv suddenly. "Call him and invite him here tomorrow morning. Tell him you understand that we have been trespassing on his land and would like to talk to him about it. He'll come, I know he will!"

The sun was beginning to appear over the tops of the trees the next morning when Mr. Vikram came to the Sukhi Rest House. As Shiv had predicted, he had quickly agreed to come over for a meeting when Sunnu had called about the supposed trespassing. That small patch of bamboo-covered land was clearly very important to him.

Jody had been keeping watch on the veranda since dawn. She hadn't slept very well, her head full of anxious thoughts about Sandhi and the poachers. She had been relieved when the sun rose and the dawn light began to filter into her bedroom. Brittany hadn't stirred when she crept out of bed and down to the veranda. She had made herself a cup of tea and had scribbled several pages in her diary before anyone else had gotten up.

Dr. Taylor had been the first to appear. He was off on a bird-watching trip to the coast with Mei Lin and Maddie. After she had waved them off, Jody had chatted with Harry and Cam aboard the *Dolphin Dreamer* for a while. And at last, Mr. Vikram's small dinghy had come into view.

As soon as she saw the boat, Jody scrambled to her feet and flew into the house. Her parents, the twins, and the Kaushik family were now up and were making breakfast in the kitchen. There was still no sign of Brittany.

"Mr. Vikram's coming!" Jody announced excitedly. "He'll be here in about ten minutes, I think."

"Well, we are ready for him," said Sunnu calmly.

"As ready as we'll ever be," agreed Ravi.

Jody ran back outside and watched as Mr. Vikram carefully maneuvered his dinghy down the river toward the Sukhi Rest House. When he finally reached the jetty, he lashed his small, rather shabby boat firmly to one of the jetty uprights. Then he hitched up the knees of his pale linen trousers and climbed up onto the jetty.

"Good morning, Mr. Vikram," said Jody cautiously. Seeing him up close again brought back unpleasant memories of being shouted at.

Mr. Vikram peered at her. "Good morning, young lady," he said. "I am here to see Shivam's parents. Are they at home, please?"

What a strange question, Jody thought as she brought Mr. Vikram into the rest house. Where else would Sunnu and Ravi be at this time of the morning?

Mr. Vikram seemed surprised at the number of people waiting for him inside. He hesitated briefly in the doorway.

"Mr. Vikram, good morning," said Ravi, stepping forward. "Allow me to introduce the McGrath family. Mr. and Mrs. McGrath have come here to study the dolphins."

Did Mr. Vikram look nervous at the mention of dolphins? Jody looked closely, but his expression gave nothing away.

"I am very pleased to meet you," he said formally, making a small bow.

"Do sit down," suggested Sunnu.

"I prefer to stand," said Mr. Vikram. "I hope this will not take long." He shifted slightly, clasping his hands behind his back. Jody decided that he reminded her of a tall, rather awkward-looking heron.

"I am here to discuss your son," continued Mr. Vikram. "I would appreciate it if he would stay away from my property. Can you give me your promise that he will do so?"

"We don't want to upset you, Mr. Vikram," Ravi said. "I think there has just been a misunderstanding about who owns the land. Of course, if Shivam is trespassing, we will speak to him about it."

Jody looked around, but Shiv was nowhere to be seen.

Mr. Vikram seemed at a loss about what to say next. "I would like your promise," he said again. "If you please. It is your role as parents to control your children."

The sound of laughter echoed from the direction of the jetty. Shiv, Ajay, and the twins were obviously playing outside.

"We can only apologize, Mr. Vikram," said Sunnu. "I'm sorry if Shiv has been a nuisance for you."

Rav cleared his throat. "There was something else we wanted to discuss with you, Mr. Vikram," he said politely. "It is a small matter of a boat. A new boat we have found, moored some way up the river. We have reason to believe it is yours."

Mr. Vikram suddenly looked wary. "A boat?" he asked. "I have my only boat outside."

Ravi shook his head. "I have spoken to Khaled at the Mongla boatyard," he said. "We know that it is yours, Mr. Vikram. And we think that maybe you know something more. Perhaps something about the poachers who have come to this area?"

Mr. Vikram quivered with anger. He drew himself up as tall as he could and stuck out his chin. "I have no new boat!" he declared loudly. "I know nothing about poachers. I do not like your questions, and I now believe that you did not bring me here to talk about your son at all. I do not appreciate being tricked!"

With those words, he swung around quickly and marched out of the rest house door.

"Oh, dear," Sunnu muttered, collapsing into one of the armchairs. "I think we offended him."

"More than likely, I think we scared him," said Craig grimly. "Did you see his face? Quick, we have to bring him back!"

They didn't have to go very far. Mr. Vikram was standing on the jetty, staring in disbelief at the empty place where his boat had been. Out in the middle of the river, Shiv was waving, a broad grin on his face. He was bobbing gently in Mr. Vikram's boat, along with Ajay, Jimmy, and Sean.

No escape . . .

Craig ran up to Mr. Vikram and touched his arm. Mr. Vikram roughly pulled away, looking fearfully into Craig's eyes.

"Please, Mr. Vikram," said Craig gently. "We are not accusing you of anything. We simply want to know if the boat is yours and if you have noticed anything strange in the area recently."

Jody held her breath.

Mr. Vikram suddenly looked defeated. "The boat is mine," he muttered after a long silence. "What of it? I have two boats. This is the Sundarbans. You must have a boat to live here."

"Then why did you lie to us?" asked Jody, stepping up beside her dad. "And why didn't you come here in your new boat instead of your old one?"

Mr. Vikram wouldn't meet her eyes. "I don't know anything about poachers," he said stubbornly.

"Is there a particular reason you don't want anyone near your land?" Craig pressed.

Mr. Vikram hesitated. "No," he said at last.

"Mr. Vikram, you must tell us the truth," said Craig. "We don't want to bring UNESCO into this, but I think that they need to know what is going on."

Mr. Vikram looked frightened. "I don't want people there!" he said passionately. "I don't want . . . They will take them away!"

"Take who away, Mr. Vikram?" asked Jody.

Mr. Vikram crumpled in front of them. "My tigers," he said. "My precious tigers."

9

June 1 — morning — on the veranda at the Sukhi Rest House
When Mr. Vikram mentioned tigers this morning, he sur-
prised everyone. It's not really the kind of conversation
you expect to have with someone you suspect of being a
poacher! His voice was full of an emotion that I don't sup-
pose poachers know much about — love. I recognized it
right away because it's how I feel about dolphins. I some-
times feel like I'd jump in front of a firing squad before I
would let anyone hurt a dolphin. I got the feeling that Mr.
Vikram felt exactly the same about tigers. And suddenly,
I decided that I liked him.

Mr. Vikram buried his face in his hands, shaking his head helplessly. A few tears trickled through his fingers and splashed on the jetty.

"Tigers?" Ravi repeated. He sounded astonished. "What have tigers got to do with this?"

Mr. Vikram just shook his head over and over again and kept his face covered with his hands.

"Come inside, Mr. Vikram," Sunnu said gently, laying her hand on his sleeve. "Come and sit down."

"Good idea," said Gina. "Let's have some tea and talk about this. There's a lot more to this situation than meets the eye, I think."

Mr. Vikram had no more fight left in him. Meekly, he followed Sunnu and Ravi into the house.

"Are you arresting Mr. Vikram?" Jimmy shouted excitedly from the boat.

"No," Craig called back severely. "But we're thinking of arresting *you*. Stealing boats, at your age! Come back to shore, boys. You've done your part, I think."

"Now," said Craig, when they all were finally seated on the veranda and Sunnu had made tea. "Do you feel up to telling us whatever is bothering you, Mr. Vikram?"

Mr. Vikram was slowly calming down. He accepted the tea Sunnu offered him, and he seemed to be thinking hard before he spoke. "I am sorry," he said stiffly. "I am emotional today. It has been a very hard time for me."

"You mentioned tigers," Jody prompted.

The fear came back into Mr. Vikram's eyes, and he looked down into his lap.

"My wife died last year," he began. "Perhaps you know this already. We had been married for ten years. The illness should not have killed her, but life had been hard for a while, and she was weak and tired." He paused and swallowed. "I felt guilty that I couldn't save her."

"It wasn't your fault," murmured Sunnu, her eyes soft with sympathy.

Mr. Vikram shook his head. "I think maybe it was," he said. "My business was failing, but I refused to give up. The shellfish were disappearing from the river, but every day I thought we would make a big catch again, like in the past. Maybe we should have gone to Mongla, and I should have found work there. But my father and my grandfather had always worked on the river, and I was too proud to leave."

"It has been a hard time for everyone in the Sundarbans," said Ravi. "Pollution, irrigation schemes upriver — the delta is changing for us all."

Jody was suddenly aware, all over again, of just how much the people in the Sundarbans depended on the river for their livelihoods.

Mr. Vikram was still talking. "I was angry when my wife died," he said. "Angry with myself and angry with the world. So when the men came and offered me money, I took it."

Jody felt a chill settle on her heart. "Men?" she echoed quietly.

Mr. Vikram looked at her. There was real sadness in his eyes. "Bad men," he said. "I am ashamed now, but at the time, I felt nothing. They took animals with my help, and they paid me well."

Thoughts of Sandhi's family rose in Jody's mind. But she pushed them down again. It was too late to help them now, she knew. Perhaps, by listening to Mr. Vikram, they would still be able to help Sandhi and the others. What did this story have to do with tigers, she wondered?

"I found Aditi two weeks after the men left," Mr. Vikram continued. "She is a Royal Bengal tiger," he added, unable to keep the pride out of his voice. "She was skin and bone when I found her trying to take food from my house. She was so weak and starving that she didn't even try to attack me. So I started to feed her. She helped me to get over the death of my wife, I think." Mr. Vikram stopped and stared out of the window. "She started to trust me."

"And Aditi is now living on that patch of land with the bamboo?" Gina asked.

Mr. Vikram nodded. "She is living there with her new family," he said. He gave his first real smile. "She had two cubs three months ago. I have been protecting her and taking food to her — just to build her strength back up."

"Is she the tiger we have been hearing these past few days?" Ravi asked suddenly.

Mr. Vikram nodded. "She has been calling loudly in

the past week — calling for her mate, I think. It made me afraid."

"But why are you afraid?" asked Gina in confusion. "You know that she won't hurt you."

Mr. Vikram raised his hands in the air. "I'm not afraid for myself, Mrs. McGrath," he said. "I am afraid for Aditi. Because the poachers are back, and I know they want to take her away."

"But are you helping the poachers again?" asked Ravi.

Mr. Vikram looked ashamed. "I don't want to," he said helplessly. "But they know about the tigers. If I don't help, they will take them away."

"Blackmail," said Craig. "Right?"

Mr. Vikram was silent. Then he nodded. "The poachers know that I will help them in order to protect Aditi and her children," he said.

"Did they give you the money to buy the boat?" asked Sunnu.

Mr. Vikram nodded again. "Yes," he whispered. "My business still isn't so good, so I have taken a little money from them."

Jody suddenly felt heart-wrenchingly sorry for Mr.

Vikram. She wondered what she would do in the same situation, if Sandhi was in danger and helping the poachers was the only way to protect her. Then she remembered that Sandhi was already in danger. Very grave danger.

"Do you trust these men?" asked Philip suddenly.

Philip hadn't been in the room the last time Jody looked. Now he was leaning back against the doorway with his art bag and stool propped up beside him. He must have come in from painting while they had been listening to Mr. Vikram.

Mr. Vikram looked taken aback. "Of course not!" he said. "They are bad men. I would be a fool if I trusted them. Even more of a fool than I am now," he added quietly.

"So what's to stop them from taking your tigers, anyway, even if you help them?" Philip continued.

Mr. Vikram opened his mouth, but no sound came out.

"Philip's right," said Gina. "I think these men will try to take Aditi and her cubs, whether you help them or not."

Mr. Vikram jumped to his feet and started pacing up and down. "But what else can I do?" he asked.

"We can help you protect the tigers," offered Jody. She looked at her dad, who nodded and smiled at her.

Mr. Vikram slowly sank back down into a chair. He looked overcome at Jody's offer. "You will help me?" he said. "Even . . . even though I, too, am a bad man?"

"You are not a bad man, Mr. Vikram," said Gina kindly. "You just made a bad mistake. Now you have a chance to make up for what you did and help us to preserve the wildlife of the river."

"But you must tell us everything you know about the poachers," added Ravi. "We must then involve UNESCO. This is a very serious matter. Do you understand?"

Mr. Vikram gave a very small nod. "Yes," he said. "I see that it is the only way. Very well. If you promise to help me protect Aditi and her family, I will tell you everything I know."

At last, the whole story came flooding out. Mr. Vikram explained that the poachers operated along much of the Sundarbans coast, preferring to move around rather than stay in one place for too long. There were three of them in the gang, and they stole animals of all kinds — crocodiles and snakes for their skin, monkeys for their fur, birds for their feathers, turtles and dolphins for their meat and oil. Jody felt sick to her stomach. She desperately wanted to ask Mr. Vikram if the poachers had taken Sandhi, but she was afraid of the answer. So she stayed silent — until Mr. Vikram made a startling announcement.

"They are meeting again tonight," he said, looking around at everyone. "At the boat."

"Tonight!" Jody gasped. Suddenly, it all felt very dangerous and very real.

"Then we will be waiting for them," said Craig grimly. "They have gotten away with it so far. But tonight is our big chance. We'll call UNESCO and tell the other people along the river. Do you think they'll help, Ravi?"

"Definitely," said Ravi quietly. "Men like these poachers are stealing from our river. We all want to stop them."

"Then that's settled," said Craig. "Tonight it is."

Jody stood on the jetty with her family and the Kaushiks and watched Mr. Vikram's boat as it headed back upriver.

"I think he is sailing his boat more happily," Shiv observed.

Jimmy laughed. "How can you sail a boat happily?" he said. "That's silly."

"Shh, Jimmy," Gina cautioned, putting her arm around him. "I know what Shiv means."

"So do I," said Jody, watching the little boat's progress. Mr. Vikram turned and waved once, before

Sailing more happily . . .

133

the boat disappeared around the bend. "Mr. Vikram knows he's not on his own anymore."

Brittany came out of the rest house, yawning and holding a cup of tea. "You're all up early," she said.

"We've been pretty busy," Jody said with a grin.

Brittany listened to the events of the morning with wide eyes, completely forgetting about her tea. "So they're coming tonight!" she gasped as Jody came to the end. "But — won't they be dangerous?"

"We'll be able to cope with them," said Jody confidently.

Craig held up his hand. "Stop right there, Jody," he said. "What's this 'we' business?"

"Dad!" Jody began, but her heart was sinking. She knew what he was about to say.

"You can forget about joining us tonight," Craig continued severely. "It'll be far too dangerous."

"Your dad's right," said Gina. "I'm sorry, Jody."

"But that's so unfair!" Jody burst out. "Shiv and I remembered about Mr. Vikram and the boat. You wouldn't even know about the poachers if we hadn't remembered!"

134

"I want to come, too!" insisted Shiv.

"Me, too!" added Sean and Jimmy in chorus.

"Me three!" That was Ajay. Jimmy had taught him the new expression that morning, and he was keen to try it out.

"We're very grateful to you and Shiv, Jody," Ravi said, holding up his hands. "But we can't allow any of you to come with us tonight. I'm sorry."

That seemed to be the end of the discussion. The adults returned to the rest house with Ajay, Ambika, and the twins, leaving Jody, Shiv, and Brittany still standing on the jetty. Jody felt so disappointed that she thought she was going to cry.

"Don't be upset, Jody," said Shiv. "You know what grown-ups are like."

Jody sighed. "I know. I shouldn't be too surprised, I guess."

"I can't believe you want to go!" said Brittany. "I mean — they might have *guns* or something."

"Hey, you three." Philip had reappeared from the rest house and was walking toward them. "We had an idea," he said when he reached them. "I know it's disappointing that you can't come tonight, but I've got a suggestion. Something that might take your mind off the poachers."

Jody didn't think anything would do that, until she heard Philip's next words.

"Why don't we go and feed Mr. Vikram's tigers tonight instead?"

10

May 31 — early evening — on the way to Bamboo Island (new name!)

I can't write much because the pages will get wet. The river's calmed down a lot since the storm, I'm pleased to say — but my writing's still a bit wobbly. We're heading for Bamboo Island with some dinner for the tigers. We picked up the meat from Mr. Vikram on our way here, and Philip put it right in the front of the boat. Shiv doesn't seem to mind, but Brittany is sitting as far away from it as possible. I can tell Philip's really excited. I guess he's finally going to see some tigers close enough to draw!

I'm trying to stay positive, but I keep seeing gray shapes rising out of the waves and thinking that maybe it's Sandhi. Feeding tigers is exciting, but I still can't stop thinking about the poachers. Will Mom and Dad be OK? They got a group of UNESCO patrol guys and a whole lot of the Kaushiks' friends together, so they have plenty of backup. Mr. Vikram said that there were only three poachers, but what if they have guns, like Brittany said?

Jody closed her diary and put it in her backpack. She was just getting more and more worried and, besides, they were nearly at Bamboo Island. Shiv was already standing up with the dinghy rope in his hands, ready to throw it over the old mangrove stump. Moping about Sandhi wasn't going to help, Jody knew. She straightened her shoulders and jumped ashore.

"I really hope these tigers are as tame as Mr. Vikram said they were," joked Philip as he offered his hand to Brittany.

Brittany held back, looking uncertain. "I think maybe I'll stay in the boat, just in case . . ." she began.

"Come on, Brittany," Jody coaxed. "Think of those lovely baby tigers. I bet they're really cute."

Brittany's eyes softened. "Do you think?" she said, stepping onto the island.

Jody half expected Mr. Vikram to jump out at them, like he had before. But the island was calm and still, with a gentle breeze swishing through the bamboo.

With the help of Shiv, Philip dragged the meat off the boat. They placed it carefully on a patch of ground close to the bamboo, as Mr. Vikram had told them.

"It's disgusting," complained Brittany, wrinkling her nose as she stared at the meat.

"Yes," Jody agreed. "But at least if we give the tigers some supper, they won't think about eating us."

"Don't say things like that, Jody," muttered Brittany, stepping back from the bamboo.

Philip and Shiv joined Jody and Brittany on the shore, wiping their hands on their trousers.

"What now?" asked Jody expectantly.

"Now we wait," said Philip, checking his watch. "I hope they come soon. The light is fading fast. It would be just my luck to get close enough to a tiger to actually sketch it, but not be able to see it properly!"

"Do you think the tigers will stay still long enough for you to *draw* them?" Brittany asked in amazement.

"A quick sketch, maybe," said Philip. He then dug into his bag and pulled out a camera. "And if they don't, at least I'll be able to get some real close-up photos." He grinned.

Jody's eyes went longingly toward the river. Her parents and the others would be setting off soon. They would pass Bamboo Island on their way to the Irrawaddy inlet. She wished she could be with them.

"Jody!" Shiv whispered at Jody's elbow. "Look!"

Jody turned to see the most amazing sight. A cautious orange-and-black-striped face had appeared at the edge of the bamboo. Aditi the tigress stared at the visitors with a haughty expression on her face, as if daring them to come closer.

When no one moved, Aditi obviously decided that it was safe to come out. She padded out of the bamboo as gracefully as a dancer. Close on her tail were two young cubs, their orange-and-black fur soft and fluffy around their inquisitive little faces. One of the cubs batted Aditi's tail and let out a small, high-pitched growl. The second cub tossed its fluffy tail, getting ready to pounce on its brother. They were behaving just like playful cats back at home, thought Jody, entranced.

Aditi sniffed the meat slowly. The cubs yowled, hungry and impatient. With one last glance at the visitors, the tigress and her youngsters settled down to eat.

Jody looked across at Philip. He was wasting no time and had already snapped several photos. Now he was drawing the tigers with swift strokes of his pencil. The tigers could disappear into the bamboo again at any moment, Jody knew. She really hoped that they would stay for a little while longer. She could hardly believe she was here, watching a family of wild tigers this close. Philip's pictures would really be something to add to the Dolphin Universe web site. She could imagine how impressed her friends would be!

After twenty minutes, Jody heard the faint purring sound of a boat engine on the river. Was it the poacher patrol? She got to her feet as slowly as she could, trying not to frighten Aditi and her cubs, and walked to the edge of the island. Peering into the darkening evening, she saw a fleet of five boats heading toward her. Soon she could make out her father, standing at the prow of the lead boat. She waved frantically and was rewarded with a return wave and a smile.

Jody saw her dad lean down and whisper something to the driver of the boat. To her surprise, the lead boat peeled off from the rest and headed toward her. In the boat were her dad, her mom, Ravi, and two men she assumed were from UNESCO.

"Just thought we'd see if you were OK —" Craig began as they got close enough to Bamboo Island to have a conversation.

Jody hastily held her finger to her lips and pointed at the feeding tigers. Five pairs of eyes widened as they met the fierce gaze of Aditi, who had looked up from the meat to examine the new visitors. No one moved for an agonizing minute. Then Aditi returned to her meal, growling softly in contentment.

"What a beautiful animal," Gina whispered after a minute. "I can't believe we're so close to her."

Suddenly, Aditi lifted her head and looked behind her. She growled again. This time, her growl was less friendly. It made the hairs on Jody's neck stand up. Aditi had heard something she didn't like. Her whole body tensed, and her cubs clustered nervously around her feet. The meat was forgotten. Something more dangerous was in the air.

Jody heard three voices speaking in Hindi. They were approaching from deep in the forest. Aditi and her cubs disappeared into the undergrowth, as silently as ghosts. Only the remains of the meat proved that the tigers had ever been there.

With a pounding heart, Jody looked across at Shiv. Three men speaking Hindi. Could it be . . . ?

"I think we're about to meet the poachers," said Craig, his voice tense.

There was a rush of activity from the boat as Gina, Craig, Ravi, and the two UNESCO men jumped ashore. Brittany gasped and grabbed Philip's arm. Jody's legs suddenly felt like lead. Why were they here? Why weren't the poachers at the Irrawaddy inlet with the boat?

"Get in your boat, now," Ravi instructed them all. "And stay quiet, OK? We'll handle this."

Jody suddenly knew this was for real. She ran to the boat, dragging Brittany with her. Shiv followed closely behind. The unthinkable had happened. They were about to meet the poachers face-to-face. How had this happened? They weren't supposed to be here! Had they come for the tigers?

Craig ran to the edge of the water. Jody watched as he waved at the remaining four boats, making urgent cutting gestures with his hand — *Cut the engines!* Quickly, the boats obeyed. In moments, the evening air was still. Very quietly, the four boats rowed into shore and anchored just off the island, ready for action.

The three men in the forest were approaching fast, crashing recklessly through the undergrowth. They seemed to be arguing with raised voices. Jody watched the unfolding scene with a sense of disbelief. This kind of thing happened in movies, not in real life.

It was just as Mr. Vikram had feared. The poachers had discovered Aditi's lair, and they were coming to get her and the cubs while Mr. Vikram was waiting to meet them at the Irrawaddy inlet!

Jody watched from the safety of the boat as three men emerged from the bamboo, still arguing. One of them held a tranquilizer gun, and another had a long wire lasso. They were so wrapped up in their conversation that they were completely taken by surprise.

"Stop right there!" shouted one of the UNESCO men. He was holding a gun and aiming it straight at the poachers.

The three poachers stopped dead. They stared at the reception committee in disbelief. Two UNESCO men from one of the backup boats ran in and quickly disarmed the man with the tranquilizer gun. Soon all three poachers were on their knees, surrounded by men in official uniforms. Radios crackled as the patrol reported the arrest. Bamboo Island was suddenly swarming with officers, and the air buzzed with fevered excitement and relief.

"Got them!" Craig came bounding up to the boat with a broad smile on his face. "Is everyone OK?"

"Yes!" Brittany shouted triumphantly. She punched the air with her hand. Shiv jumped out of the boat and hurried over to his parents, who hugged him warmly.

Jody suddenly felt a bit trembly. Now that it was all over, she realized just how dangerous it could have been.

"Jody?" asked Craig. "How are you holding up?"

"I'm glad you got them," Jody said unsteadily, emotions welling up and threatening to overwhelm her. Then she burst out, "But Dad, I'm more glad that you're safe!"

June 1 — morning — aboard Dolphin Dreamer
It's almost eleven o'clock already, and we only got up an hour ago. I think the excitement of last night wore us out. I don't remember much about the boat ride home, except that Mom and Dad were sitting next to me and holding my hands. It felt really strange coming back to the normality of the Sukhi Rest House. Everything felt so down to earth. I didn't even want supper. I just crashed in bed. Brittany did, too.

So now we're all having a celebration breakfast

aboard Dolphin Dreamer — *all the Kaushiks, Philip, the whole* Dolphin Dreamer *team, and a few UNESCO guys. Mei Lin has made mango muffins with some of Dr. Taylor's fruit!*

I think we've met every single person in the Sundarbans today. They've all been dropping by, congratulating us and thanking us for our help. Mr. Vikram didn't come, though. He told the police everything, and Dad said he probably won't go to prison. He will need to go and stay in Mongla for the trial, though, so Philip promised to keep an eye on Aditi and the cubs. Philip's started a painting now, and he needs a whole lot of new sketches. He won't have to rely on his photos after all!

I'm pleased that they've caught the poachers, obviously. But we still haven't found out about the one Irrawaddy dolphin I most wanted to see. Mom told me this morning to expect the worst about Sandhi, as stolen animals don't usually turn up again.

Jody stared out at the river, her diary open by her side. The sky was blue, and the water glinted and swirled around *Dolphin Dreamer* as she bobbed gently with the current. It was soothing to be on board again. They were planning to leave the Sundarbans in two days. Jody knew that there would be new adventures to distract her from thoughts of Sandhi and her family, but right now, she couldn't get excited about it.

Brittany came and sat next to Jody, holding two plates of mango muffins and banana bread. "You're missing the breakfast," she said, offering Jody one of the plates. "I had to fight Dr. Taylor for these. He was going back for a third helping!"

"Thanks, Brittany," Jody said. "But I don't want anything right now."

Brittany put the plate on the table. "Well, it's there if you change your mind," she said with a shrug. Then she got up and walked over to talk to Philip on the far side of the deck.

Jody turned back to stare at the river again, trying to ignore the cheerful chatter on the deck. A couple of crocodiles were sunning themselves on the riverbank with their mouths wide open. Several little birds stood beside them and picked at their teeth like small white dentists. Deep in the jungle, she could hear the endless chatter and screech of the monkeys. The whole forest was alive. Now all she needed was for the small gray shape bobbing beside *Dolphin Dreamer* to turn magically into Sandhi, and the world would be perfect.

The small gray shape disappeared under the waves, then reappeared. Jody blinked and half rose from her chair. She stared into the water. There it was again! She had definitely seen a dorsal fin this time. She didn't dare let herself get too hopeful. Maybe it was Susie the Ganges River dolphin? But there was no sign of Susie's distinctive beak.

With mounting excitement, Jody pulled herself right up against the railing and peered down into the water. One head, then another smaller one appeared in the river.

"Mom!" She gasped. "Dad! Shiv! Come quick! I think Sandhi's back!"

Gina came over. "I told you not to get your hopes up, Jody," she began.

"There!" said Jody, pointing. Happiness threatened to choke her. "It's Sandhi, see? And I think she's got a baby with her!"

Sandhi's grave little face bobbed up to the surface of the river. Beside her was the much smaller, paler head of a calf.

"It looks like the poachers didn't get her after all!" Gina breathed. "She must have gone away to have her baby in privacy. What a clever mom!"

Jody stared deep into Sandhi's eyes. The dolphin's expression was soft and understanding, as if she knew

Sandhi has a surprise for me!

that Jody had been worrying. *Stay safe, Sandhi,* Jody thought. *The poachers have gone now, so you and your baby will be fine.*

Her heart was full to bursting. Suddenly, the merry chatter of the celebration breakfast aboard *Dolphin Dreamer* seemed perfectly in tune with her soaring mood. She'd never seen such a beautiful forest, or such lovely people, or such a gorgeous morning as this one. "Where are those muffins?" she demanded, looking around. "I'm starving!"

Sandhi bobbed on the surface of the river as everyone gathered around the railings of *Dolphin Dreamer* to watch her and her calf. She seemed to be enjoying the attention. In fact, her solemn little face looked like it would break into a smile at any minute.

MORE SERIES YOU'LL FALL IN LOVE WITH

TWITCHES

Imagine finding out you have an identical twin. Cam and Alex just did. Think nothing can top that? Guess again. (They also just learned they're witches.)

Take one big city—New York. Add three very different girls—Carolyn, Maya and Joy. Bake all summer long. Result? Real problems, real friendship, real fun.

Heartland™

Nestled in the foothills of Virginia, there's a place where horses come when they are hurt. Amy, Ty, and everyone at Heartland work together to heal the horses—and form lasting bonds that will touch your heart.

**Learn more at
www.scholastic.com/books**

Available Wherever Books Are Sold.

■ SCHOLASTIC

GIRLT3

Friends and adventures that set your heart free.

❏ 0-439-31947-1	Dolphin Diaries #1: Into the Blue	$4.99 US
❏ 0-439-31948-X	Dolphin Diaries #2: Touching the Waves	$4.99 US
❏ 0-439-31949-8	Dolphin Diaries #3: Riding the Storm	$4.99 US
❏ 0-439-31950-1	Dolphin Diaries #4: Under the Stars	$4.99 US
❏ 0-439-31951-X	Dolphin Diaries #5: Chasing the Dream	$4.99 US
❏ 0-439-31952-8	Dolphin Diaries #6: Racing the Wind	$4.99 US
❏ 0-439-44614-7	Dolphin Diaries #7: Following the Rainbow	$4.99 US
❏ 0-439-44615-5	Dolphin Diaries #8: Dancing the Seas	$4.99 US
❏ 0-439-44616-3	Dolphin Diaries #9: Leaving the Shallows	$4.99 US

Available wherever you buy books, or use this order form.

Scholastic Inc., P.O. Box 7502, Jefferson City, MO 65102

Please send me the books I have checked above. I am enclosing $_____ (please add $2.00 to cover shipping and handling). Send check or money order — no cash or C.O.D.s please.

Name_____ Birth date_____

Address_____

City_____ State/Zip_____

Please allow four to six weeks for delivery. Offer good in U.S.A. only. Sorry, mail orders are not available to residents of Canada. Prices subject to change.

www.scholastic.com

DDBL0504